Carter calmly flipped a table and smashed it down over the man's head.

"That's enough!"

Carter turned. The barman had moved out. He stood now in front of the bar, holding a gun.

By the time the nervous gun fired, Carter was already too close and dived under the slug.

He shouldered the gun to the side before a second shot could be fired, and filled the man's belly with his right fist.

The gun fell to the floor. Carter gave him a fast right, then a knee in the gut that straightened him up against the bar. Then he measured him and mashed his beetlike nose all over his face . . .

NICK CARTER IS IT!

FROM THE NICK CARTER
KILLMASTER SERIES

NICK CARTER

KILLMASTER

Tunnel for Traitors

CHARTER BOOKS, NEW YORK

TUNNEL FOR TRAITORS

A Charter Book/published by arrangement with
The Condé Nast Publications, Inc.

PRINTING HISTORY
Charter edition/June 1986

ISBN: 0-441-57283-9

Charter Books are published by The Berkley Publishing Group,
200 Madison Avenue, New York, New York 10016.
PRINTED IN THE UNITED STATES OF AMERICA

*Dedicated to·the men of the
Secret Services of the
United States of America*

ONE

The sun was a molten, golden ball over Nassau. Between it and the earth a heavy heat haze shimmered, giving everything the eye looked upon an eerie, mirage-like quality.

In the back of the cab, Nick Carter squinted behind dark glasses and casually checked over his shoulder through the rear window.

There was no reason for a tail. He was on vacation, or was supposed to be. Just a weekend of sun and gambling.

He checked anyway. It was a habit of the survivor who wanted to stay alive a while longer in a deadly game.

West Bay Street narrowed and the houses gave way to a wide, white beach littered with straw umbrellas and sun-worshiping bodies. A zigzag in the road brought the cab to the British Colonial Hotel. She was a stately old pink dowager, right on the water and surrounded by beautiful gardens.

"This is fine," Carter told the driver, preferring to walk the few remaining blocks to Rowson's Square and the Café Olanda. If they had eyes and ears on him, he should have spotted them by now.

When he reached Prince George Wharf he paused,

admiring a couple of luxury liners docked for the day, and then did a three-sixty with his eyes while casually lighting a cigarette.

Chattering tourists, straw vendors, and a few clip-clopping horse-drawn carriages made up the landscape around the harbor.

And then he saw him: fat, sporting white trousers, a wide-brimmed straw hat, and a T-shirt two sizes too small for his expanding gut. He sat at the outside terrace of the Olanda trying desperately to look cool and comfortable.

No one in his right mind would sit outside at this time of day. No one, that is, except someone who was waiting and watching for someone else.

So, Carter thought, rather than tail him from the hotel, they had just decided to sit at the appointed place and wait.

Carter flipped his cigarette away and moved across the street. The man in white checked him once and moved his eyes back to the street.

The Killmaster took a table in the depths of the café under a revolving fan and ordered a rum cooler.

He figured the man would take twenty minutes to check him for a tail. He used up fifteen before he grunted himself to his feet, curled a newspaper under his arm, and waddled away.

Carter sipped his drink, lit a cigarette, and settled back to wait.

He was going to see her again after all these years. He wondered if she would be as youthful, as beautiful, as appealing as he remembered.

He doubted it.

But he hoped she was.

Her name was Trena Klassen. Back then, when Carter had first met her, she had been a young clerk in East Germany's world trade commission. She, and her brother Klaus, were also West German ''sleeper'' agents. As such, they had helped Carter expose and terminate a very dangerous Soviet double agent.

Now Klaus was a high mucky-muck with the East

German secret police, and Trena had an equally important position on the trade commission.

Two weeks earlier she had contacted Macron Limited's West German offices. Her people were interested in buying some sophisticated laser mirrors from the company's home factory in California.

It was an alert code. Trena had something to pass, something important enough that it needed passing one-on-one.

Because Carter knew her on sight, he had been chosen to make the meet. The Bahamas had been selected because it was neutral ground close to Cuba, where Trena would be attending a trade conference.

Macron, of course, was a company that existed only on paper. It was used for many things, its lure to the Soviets the fact that it supposedly manufactured many of the high-tech instruments so badly needed by the Russian industrial machine.

Carter was representing Macron as Clyde Moran, a research and development expert.

And then she was there, standing on the sidewalk by the ring of tables, turning her head, searching the interior of the café for the sign.

She looked magnificent. Her blond hair was coiled atop her head, her large eyes were only faintly made up, and her lips still held the slight pout he remembered so well.

If possible, her figure was even more sensual and tantalizing. Her firm breasts strained every thread of a thin knit top. Her hips, still wide but nicely rounded, were encased in a skin-hugging skirt. They swung provocatively as she moved through the tables.

Carter had already broken two unlit cigarettes and arranged them in the ashtray to form a diamond shape.

She spotted it, and headed directly for him. Inches from the table, she stopped and Carter stood.

"Trena, how nice to see you again after all these years."

The addition of a padded jaw, a mustache, and some

gray in the hair had fooled her. But the voice she recognized instantly. She went white and one hand went up to her breasts.

Carter covered by embracing her and kissing each cheek. He paused with his lips by her ear.

"Cool it, luv, you're supposed to be a business acquaintance, remember?"

"I didn't know they were sending you," she whispered in reply.

"We should both be used to old lovers showing up in our line of work."

He backed off, and she sat rather heavily in the chair. Carter resumed his seat and poured a glass of water, which she grabbed.

"I saw your errand boy."

"He was making sure you weren't followed."

"I know, for my own safety. We American industrialists who scheme to avoid the export laws can't be too careful." The waiter appeared. "The lady will have one of these."

The man nodded and moved away.

"What is it?" she asked, eyeing the glass.

"Rum."

"I hate rum."

"When in Rome," Carter said with a shrug, then lit a fresh cigarette. "You're still very beautiful."

"On the outside, perhaps," Trena sighed. "On the inside, I'm about burned out." Her eyes appraised him thoughtfully. "The years have been good to you."

"It's the makeup."

The waiter deposited the drink and left. Carter leaned forward and dropped his voice even lower.

"You must have a hot one."

"I do . . . in fact it's burning. Do you know Alderstaadt?"

Carter's brows knitted in concentration. "Vaguely. It's

a little village that was split almost directly in half by the Berlin Wall.''

''Yes. There was a huge underground bunker built there during the war. Klaus has found out that the bunker has been renovated.''

''So?''

''So, it is being made into a telephone junction, a terminus, completely automated, that will handle over a thousand calls simultaneously, as well as a computer in East Berlin, as well as in and out of the country.''

''Jesus . . .''

''And the concrete side of the bunker is only sixty feet from the wall.''

Carter's eyes widened, and he allowed himself a slight gasp. ''Could it be breached?''

''Klaus thinks so.''

''What a coup . . .''

''Exactly. I have the keys to the alarm system and the master of the connections on microdots.''

''Are we being watched?''

''Of course, and I had to be very careful in the method I used to get them out of East Berlin.''

Carter smiled. ''Then we'll have to meet later.''

''Yes, for a swim. I'll tell my two keepers that you want more than just money to consummate our bargain.''

''Will they buy that?''

Her eyes clouded and flickered away from his. He understood at once. It wouldn't be the first time Trena had used her body in the course of her job.

''I understand,'' he said softly.

''I thought you would,'' she replied, and then grinned. ''But I am glad they sent you.''

''So am I. How do we make the switch?''

''You're at the Cable Beach Resort?''

''I'm sure your watchers have already told you that.''

''Of course. I'm right next door, at Wyndam's Ambassador Beach. Tonight, take a midnight swim out to the breakwater. But first go to a little shop just down from here on Bay Street and buy a bikini. The shop is called Dione's.''

''Buy . . .''

''A picture of it is attached under my side of the table with two-sided tape.''

Carter nodded. ''A replacement?''

''Yes.'' She stood and paused. ''Midnight?''

''Midnight.''

''By the way, I wear a size eight.''

She turned and walked toward the entrance. From the back, as she moved across the café, she was just as beautiful as she was from the front.

The fat man in white materialized from somewhere outside the café and followed her at a distance.

Carter waited several minutes to make sure a second one wasn't watching him before he felt beneath the table.

It was an ad from a West German fashion magazine, in color.

Fifteen minutes later he was in the shop.

''The bikini in the window . . . the red one with all the straps and the doodads on the . . .''

''Bra.''

''Yeah. Size eight.''

Wrapped, it looked no bigger than a doughnut.

''One hundred and twenty-five dollars, sir.''

''One hundred . . . for *that*?''

''It's very fashionable, sir.''

''Yeah, yeah, I'll bet it is.''

He paid, slipped the package in his pocket, and left the shop.

Better in the Bahamas? Bullshit, he thought as he hailed a cab back to his hotel.

They reached the breakwater simultaneously. Carter crawled to the top and turned to give her a hand.

He need not have bothered. She had hoisted herself to the top right beside him and was already tugging at the top of her bikini. Her breasts had barely spilled free when her hands made the rest of the skimpy suit disappear.

She stood in front of him, totally naked. Her body was perfect, her breasts full and lush, the nipples hard and throbbing. Her skin was soft and firm. It looked like silk, and it almost seemed to glow with an inner, luminous heat.

"God, you're beautiful," he whispered.

"As desirable as I once was?" she murmured.

"Even more so," he replied in a husky voice.

Her deft hands found his own suit, and he felt it slip down his legs. Then she was stretched across the grassy center atop the breakwater and tugging him down beside her.

"Do you still want me, Nick?"

"Is there any doubt?" he replied, inching forward until his hardness pressed against her belly with an urgency she couldn't mistake.

His eyes devoured her willing body. The tips of her breasts were pink and alive, protruding from their soft mounds, erect and excited. His eyes followed the curve of her waist and reached the rise of her hip, then traveled inward along the triangle that dipped into her smooth thighs. Her stomach was flat and had a firmness that told of muscles developed just beneath the skin; her whole body had that firmness to it, soft to look at and to touch, but conditioned to a surprising toughness.

"Please," she breathed, looking up at him, "take me."

He was aware of his hardness as her eyes searched his body too, encircling an arm around her waist, drawing her to him. They stayed that way, their bodies pressed together, enjoying each other's warmth, relaxing into one another.

He kissed her gently at first, but her body and her lips

told him she wanted more, much more.

His hand swept down her naked back and found her buttocks. Pulling her tight against him, he maneuvered himself into the soft dampness between her thighs.

"Yes," she moaned, "and don't worry about making it last . . . it won't have to."

He heard her sigh as their bodies filled each other's, their skin joining. His fingers touched the sensitive base of her spine, and her long fingers reached down to touch him in the same place, then traveled farther to the back of his legs. He could feel her stretching against him, and suddenly her legs parted and he was inside her, reveling in the white-hot heat and wild desire that consumed them both.

She turned onto her back and he rose above her, kissing her face and neck, her closed eyes. Her smile was inward, but she suddenly put an arm around his neck to pull his cheek against hers, to let him know she was sharing their pleasure. Her other hand was gently insistent, drawing him into her. He paused, then advanced slowly. He sank farther, pausing again when she gasped. She urged him on, pushing upward with her hips.

His weight bore down on her, and their mutual desire became exquisitely intolerable. It was no time to linger, no time to tease. Now they needed to climb and reach their peak, to find release for screaming sensations. He thrust into her and she met and countered his movements with equal force, her fingers crooked and pressing into his skin, her knees raised slightly, her thighs squeezing against him.

His passion grew even more and he felt the nerve-tingling tension begin its ascent, all the senses in his body drawn to that one region. The same was happening to her. Her mouth was open, lips drawn back from her teeth. Her eyes were tightly shut and short gasps escaped her lips. Her muscles stiffened and juices inside her began to flow, until they burst through and flowed freely.

"Trena," he gasped as he erupted and felt her body answer.

They lay naked on the breakwater, droplets from the crystal-clear sea still dripping from their bodies. She moved and Carter could feel more of her warmth press against him. Now her hand was again drifting over him. He hardly stirred, so gentle was its caress, so light its play across his flesh. As he enjoyed the light exploration of his body, the intoxicating delights of the last half hour flowed back over him.

He rolled to his side to face her, his lips curving into a smile.

"You're amused?"

"I'm reliving."

"Was I different?"

"Yes. Even better."

She laughed, a small chuckle from deep inside her. "We've both ripened a bit with age."

He brushed the tip of her nose with his lips and slid his hand over the voluptuous curve of her hip. "Do you think they'll ever let you and your brother come out?"

She shrugged. "Not as long as we can supply the kind of information we have so far." She sighed and her eyes met his. "And that brings us to business. Besides the communications terminus, I must tell you about Copperhead."

"Copperhead?"

"A sleeper, a mole, in the West German government. He was activated about six months ago, and all the material he's passed so far has been pure gold. I'm only glad that Klaus and I are controlled through your people and not the West Germans. If we were known to the BfV or BND, I think we would be blown by now."

Carter felt her tense in his arms. In the game they played, Trena, and others like her, played the most dangerous part. They were under it twenty-four hours, and with little or no respite from the constant fear and danger of exposure.

"Are you sure it's a man?"

"No. It could be a woman. Klaus has seen much of the information passed. He thinks Copperhead is on the liaison team between your military and the BfV."

"That could be one of a number of people."

"I know. But each day Copperhead gets more dangerous. He must be brought down, and quickly, or our whole network in the East could collapse."

"I'll work on it along with the communications info you've passed."

"You bought the bikini?"

He nodded, and then smiled. "It's there, with my suit. I had it wrapped around my waist."

Trena traded the bits of material near her leg for the identical suit Carter had brought, and handed them to him.

"I suppose I must go now."

The way she said it and moved away from him to a sitting position told him that it was the last thing she wanted to do.

"You don't want to go back, do you," he said softly.

"No, but I will."

She was slumped, as though embarrassed by having revealed a weakness in herself. He looked at her striking profile in the moon's dim light, the blond, shoulder-length sweep of her drying hair, the pale lips slightly parted.

He had been in the game long enough to know when an agent was cracking from pressure.

Trena was definitely on the edge.

He debated suggesting that she defect right now. But he knew that was impossible. There was Klaus, her brother, still in the East, and the intelligence they would need once the telephone lines were tapped.

Once in, it's hard to get out.

She sat with her hands crossed on her knees, the tiny

bikini a ball of darkness in her lap. Her long-lashed eyes rested on the bobbing stern light of a small boat in the adjoining bay.

Then she was talking again, her voice so low he could barely hear her.

"Have you ever stopped to think how ludicrous are most of the things we do?"

"About all the time."

"Even making love to cover giving you microdots in the bra cups of a bikini. If you think about it real hard, it becomes downright silly."

"Then don't think about it," Carter said, reaching for her.

She eluded him and stood. Calmly, a mask of cool, calculated hardness replaced the softness in her face, and she tugged the bottom of the tiny suit over her full hips.

"The laser mirrors will come through the usual way?"

"Yes, Montreal to Amsterdam. They'll be transferred to your agent there."

"And of course they will be pitted and unusable."

"Of course."

Her full breasts disappeared beneath the bra, and she stretched into the straps.

"Good-bye, Nick."

"Trena . . ."

"Yes?"

"Copperhead . . . I'll get him."

"Let's hope so."

She turned and her lithe body knifed into the water. She surfaced and began a long-reaching crawl toward the beach and the distant lights of Wyndam's Ambassador Beach Hotel.

As she became a blur in the distance, Carter wondered if he would ever see her again . . . alive.

TWO

Carter checked into the BOQ at Templehof as a colonel in the U.S. Army Corps of Engineers. He dropped his bags and then reported to the commanding officer, General Harley Wells.

The general had already been briefed by Washington. Carter would have a free hand.

"Majors Wilson and Hardin have been assigned to you. Wilson for construction, Hardin as your communications expert. I'll okay whatever requests for material come across my desk."

"Thank you, sir. Does anyone else know who I . . .?"

"Besides myself, Hardin, and Wilson, no one. Even generals follow orders, Colonel. Good luck."

Obviously, General Wells's orders had been as specific as Carter's. And chances were good they had originated at the same source: David Hawk's offices in the Amalgamated Press and Wire Services Building on Dupont Circle in D.C.

"Follow the whole thing through all the way, Nick," Hawk had said. "Get this Copperhead bastard, and find a way to get to the terminus and tap it. I'll pave the way for you."

Carter was issued a uniform, slipped into army files, and was on a military aircraft to Frankfurt six hours later.

The microdots had been meticulously lifted from Trena's bikini and blown up. The AXE lab boys and planners had taken them apart over and over again until a plan had been conceived.

If it worked, it would be a gold mine.

"Colonel Carter?"

"Yeah?"

"Barnes, sir, Tech Three. I'm your driver."

"Do you know the Hasselbad Center . . . Corps of Engineers?"

"I do, sir."

"Let's go."

"The Jeep's this way."

It was an hour's ride, three quarters of the way across teeming West Berlin in noonday traffic.

"Grab yourself a beer and some lunch, Sergeant. This will probably take a while."

"Yes, sir."

He was breezed through the outer area and into an area that had been set aside as his own work space.

"Good afternoon, Colonel. I'll be your aide . . . Lieutenant Marino."

Her handshake was firm, like the rest of her under the green army uniform. She was a healthy-looking woman, in her late twenties, Carter guessed, with close-cropped black hair. Her nose was arched with wide nostrils, and her eyes were as black as her hair, and alert.

Carter guessed that she had never been considered beautiful by other women, probably because of her voluptuous proportions, but she was a handsome woman.

"Good afternoon, Lieutenant. Have you got a first name?"

She blinked but replied in the same businesslike tone she had used to introduce herself. "Louise, Colonel."

"Okay, Louise, I'm Nick. We won't have time for military Mickey Mouse. Where's my office?"

"Right through there, sir . . . uh, Nick."

He liked her smile. "Send Wilson and Hardin in as soon as they get here."

"They're already here, sir . . . in your office."

"Even better. Send out for some coffee, some sandwiches, some ice, and a quart of good scotch."

"Scotch?"

"That's whiskey, Louise."

"I know, sir, but . . ."

He closed the door on the rest of what she said, and moved quickly to the desk. The two young officers sitting near it rose the instant he entered the room.

They started to salute. Carter waved it away and dropped the briefcase on the desk.

"I haven't been in the army for twenty years and both of you know it, so in here we can dispense with that crap. Which one of you is Jim Wilson?"

"Me . . . uh, sir."

"It's Nick. Here."

Wilson was a sandy-haired, square-jawed hulk who looked like a refugee from the Green Bay Packers linebacker corps.

He took the six-inch-thick folder from Carter, hefted it, and read the cover: CONSTRUCTION—OPERATION CROWN PRINCE—JAMES T. WILSON—FOR YOUR EYES ONLY: ULTRA TOP SECRET.

The big man whistled. "I always wanted to be a spook."

"Welcome to the fun and games," Carter said with a chuckle. "Steve Hardin?"

"That's me."

Hardin was tall and lean, with intense gray eyes behind aviator frames. He had dark wavy hair, a hollow-cheeked face, and he sucked on a pipe in such a way that he gave

Carter the impression of being a college professor with grit.

"You've been partially briefed," Carter said, dropping into the chair behind the desk. "Let's go to work."

The AXE planning boys had done one hell of a job. The two army experts could find only a few small holes in it.

Basically, it was a simple plan, in three phases.

The shell of a building would be constructed on the western side of the wall. It would be just that, a shell, under which a tunnel could be dug from its center, under the wall, to the communications terminus.

"We'll need a pretty big diversion over there, topside, when we start drilling through the side of the bunker," Wilson offered. "Even that deep underground, with the alarm system bypassed, we'll be raising some hell."

"You'll have it," Carter said, and turned to Hardin. "Can your boys handle the tapping?"

"I can do it myself, but I'll need a three-man team. It's tricky. I think I'd rather use your people if they're available when the time comes."

"They'll be available," Carter replied. "Jim, do you agree with the dirt removal?"

The big man nodded. "Sure. We bring Steve's decoders, receivers, and recorders into the building in boxes, and take the dirt out in the empties. One thing, though . . ."

"Yeah?"

"Why mark the boxes as 'Radar Equipment'?"

"Because we want their spooks on this side to think we're building just another radar station. Steve, I'll want a lot of phony discs and antennae on the roof for that very reason."

"Will do."

"Okay, how soon can we get on it? . . . Jim?"

"Set the plans, get a team with top-secret clearance,

requisition materials, lay out the site . . . I'd say a week.''

"Good. Let's go check out the site. Oh, one more thing . . ."

"Yes?"

"Who assigned Lieutenant Marino to me?"

Wilson shrugged.

Hardin thought for a moment, then replied, "She probably came out of the officer pool right here."

"Has she got clearance?"

"I would imagine," Hardin said, and then he snapped his fingers. "If she needed ultra, she probably came from Intelligence at Spandgarten."

"Okay, you two go ahead. I'll meet you outside in a couple of minutes."

The two officers left. Carter waited a minute, then pressed the intercom.

"Yes, sir?"

"Come in for a minute, will you, Louise?"

She popped through the door in seconds.

"Yes, sir . . . Nick."

"What are you doing for dinner tonight?"

"I . . . uh, nothing, I guess."

"Good. How about the Maître on Meinekestrasse, about ten?"

"Uh, well . . . yes."

"Something wrong?"

"No, I've just never eaten at the Maître. It's not a place you frequent on a lieutenant's pay."

Carter plastered the most charming smile he could muster on his tanned face. "I'm a colonel, remember?"

"Sure . . . uh, Nick."

"Good, Louise," he said, still grinning as he guided her by the elbow back to the outer office. "By the way, where are you from in the States?"

"New Orleans."

"Then you'll love the Maître."

He left her staring after him, and joined Wilson and Hardin in the Jeep.

"Do you know Alderstaadt, Sergeant?"

"Yes, sir."

It took all three of them over an hour to agree on the site, and then Carter suggested a beer in a nearby café. They were barely seated beneath the outer awning when he excused himself.

Inside, he asked the bartender, *"Telefon, bitte?"*

A grunt, a nod, and, *"Ja."*

"Danke."

Carter dialed the memorized number and got an immediate connection. He heard the scrambler click in just as the voice came on.

"Yes?"

"N3, Code Red, Jacobs."

"Yes, sir."

A few more clicks, a whir, and Marty Jacobs, AXE head honcho for West Berlin, was on the line.

"What do you need, Nick?"

Carter liked that, no fooling around with needless hellos.

"You have the dossiers?"

"Yeah, seven of them . . . five men, two women."

"You're sure that's all the liaison people?"

"Every one of them that has any possible access to the kind of poop you're talking about."

"Good. I'll be dining at the Maître tonight with a young lady. Can you make delivery then?"

"The usual way?"

"Yeah. As soon as I go over them, I'll probably need a surveillance team. How many can you spare me?"

"The big man says give you what you need."

"Thanks. And, Marty, one more thing . . ."

"Yeah?"

"Get me everything you can on one Lieutenant Louise

Marino, U.S. Army. I want to know it all, here and in the States, right down to when she was in her momma's belly. She hails from New Orleans, if that helps speed things up.''

"No problem.''

"How long will it take?''

"Twenty-four hours if she's clean, a little longer if she's dirty.''

"That'll do. See you tonight.''

He went back out to the terrace and sat between the two majors.

"The head's gone from your beer.''

"Sorry, had to make a phone call,'' Carter replied with a grin. "Spook stuff. To the Crown Prince.''

"To the Prince,'' both men replied, and all three of them drained their steins.

THREE

Carter was twenty minutes late on purpose. Lieutenant Louise Marino had already arrived and had been seated at the table Carter had reserved earlier.

She was dressed in an off-the-shoulder basic black number that confirmed the Killmaster's assessment of her figure. It was draped low in front and hugged the rest of her with insouciance.

"Sorry I'm late—had a go-round with Washington."

She shrugged. "I've been out with senior officers before."

She said it as though all senior officers were a pain in the ass. In Carter's book that gave her a check on the credit side.

He ordered snails baked with butter and garlic as an appetizer, an entree of veal kidneys, and a bottle of quality Castell. All of this was done in perfect French.

"Your French is excellent," she commented. "How did you know the waiter would speak it?"

"It's a French restaurant," Carter shrugged, then grinned. "Besides, I've eaten here before."

"Are you trying to impress me?"

"Yes."

While they drank their aperitifs, Carter held back, let-

21

ting her steer the conversation. She obliged, not too subtly trying to worm personal background out of him.

Carter countered with an off-the-top-of-his-head fabrication that he knew she couldn't check.

The only reason he was suspicious of her was the fact that General Wells had not mentioned assigning her to him. He had called the general about it, and the reply was unsatisfactory.

"Probably matter of course," Wells had said. "You're a senior officer on temporary assignment. You require an office, you get a secretary aide. But I'll check on it."

Halfway through the entree she switched the questioning to the project.

"You're very curious, aren't you," Carter countered.

"Why not? If I'm to be part of something, I think I should know what it is."

It was the right answer, but it was delivered with a bit of a nervous tic at one corner of her pretty mouth.

If she were playing spy, or even amateur snoop for someone, Carter thought, she wasn't very good at it.

He threw her another curve. "Who assigned you to me?"

Her eyes danced a little too much avoiding his, and the veal trembled slightly on her fork.

"General Headquarters," she blurted. "I work out of a pool. We're assigned to all transient incoming officers."

"Oh? More wine?" He poured without waiting for an answer. "I suppose you really should know what we're up to. It's a new radar station."

He embroidered the radar station scam with a lot of technical gobbledygook that she seemed to accept. By the time they got to the dessert of fresh fruit dipped in liqueur-flavored dark chocolate, she was just a pretty girl out on a date with a strange man.

Marty Jacobs arrived over brandy and coffee, and was seated in one of the small adjoining dining rooms. Carter spotted him loping along behind the maître d' just before he disappeared.

Jacobs was easy to spot. He was tall, thin, and wiry, with a homely face that one immediately found likable. His busy brows, pale blue eyes, and shock of wild hair made him look very American and far more boyish than he really was.

The woman with him was conservatively dressed in a gray suit, her dark hair gathered in a chignon at the back of her head. Carter didn't recognize her, but he knew who she was.

Five minutes later, Jacobs's "date" rose and moved through the main dining room to the *Damen* toilette. Carter reached for the matches on the table, and over went the nearly empty wine bottle.

"Damn! I'm sorry, Louise—how clumsy of me—"

"It's only a small spot and the dress is black," she replied, fending off two solicitous waiters and dabbing at her lap with a napkin.

"The rest room attendant can spot-clean and dry it before it does too much damage," Carter insisted.

"No, it's—"

"Mein Herr is right, Fräulein," one of the waiters interjected. "The ladies' room attendant can take care of it in just a few minutes."

Before Louise could object further, Carter had her up and turned toward the rear of the room. "Oh . . . your purse . . ."

She stalked away, more annoyed than embarrassed, and Carter resumed his seat. He lit a cigarette and slitted his eyes in reverie, as if he were actually looking through the walls before him.

Both the attendant and the other woman in the gray suit would be most helpful. Louise would be ensconced in the waiting area and her dress removed.

While the attendant tended to the dress, Louise would

discover that the woman in the suit was also American, a tourist in Berlin for the first time.

Conversation would turn to the clumsiness of some men and the excitement of living in Berlin as part of the military.

The attendant would bustle back in with the dress, and while it was being slipped over Louise's head, the other woman would drop a small chrome cylinder no larger than a lipstick into Louise's purse.

Carter called for and paid the check.

The whole operation took fifteen minutes and Louise was back at the table.

"It's still wet."

"Hmmm, well, we'll just have to raincheck the evening of Berlin nightlife I had planned. Come along, I'll cab you home."

She lived in her own apartment in the Heiligensee section.

"Nice neighborhood," Carter drawled, stepping from the cab.

And it was, a very nice neighborhood on a lieutenant's pay. There were several blocks of well-tended brick brownstones, their front stoops scrubbed to a sheen. Here and there Carter could see huge old Victorian-style houses that had escaped the Allied battering during World War II.

Against her objections, he paid the cab and guided her toward the front door.

"Just a nightcap," he said and smiled. "And besides, I need to use your bathroom."

The apartment was a fourth-story floor-through, clean and modestly furnished.

"I'll fix the drinks," he said, heading for a sideboard that obviously doubled as a bar.

"I thought you were in a rush."

"Ladies first."

He followed her out of the corner of his eye as she walked through the bedroom. Just as he'd hoped, she dropped her wrap and purse on the corner of the bed.

He was tempted to do it right then, but decided to wait.

There was a small sofa, two chairs, and a coffee table arranged before the fireplace. It was on a side of the room that had the inner part of the bedroom hidden from view.

He set the drinks on the coffee table and waited. When she reappeared, he headed for the bedroom.

"Why don't you put on some music?" he murmured in passing.

"It's late. Work in the morning, remember?"

"Sure . . . okay."

He made sure she had settled into one of the chairs before he passed through the door.

It didn't take long. Instead of digging in the bottomless pit of her purse, he dumped the contents on the bed. With the cylinder palmed, he quickly scooped everything back into the bag and went on into the bathroom.

He had the names, photographs, backgrounds, and security clearances of the entire West German liaison force, and all without meeting—and taking a chance on being spotted with—Marty Jacobs.

Two minutes later he was back in the living room chatting about the project and the work they would be doing together in the next few weeks.

Just as he'd predicted, Louise forgot about trying to get rid of him so early.

He picked his time carefully, waiting until they were down to specifics about the building and its use, before making his move.

"I think we'd be much more comfortable talking in the bedroom, Louise."

As he spoke, he tugged her gently to her feet and wrapped his arms around her.

"Colonel . . ."

His lips ground over hers and he slid one hand down over the full curve of her backside.

She mumbled angrily and twisted her face from his. When he tugged her harder against him, she resisted.

"What the hell are you doing . . .?" she sputtered.

"Come on, honey . . ."

She had a good right hand. It landed on the side of his head, filling the room with a loud *thwack*.

"You bastard!"

"Sorry," he said, stepping back. "I guess I misread the signs."

"You're damned right you did!"

Carter got as humble as possible, apologized again, profusely, and headed for the door.

So much for that, he thought. If Louise Marino wanted information at any cost, she would not have hesitated taking him to bed in hopes of getting it.

Nevertheless, he stopped a block from her building and moved into a darkened doorway.

Just in case, he thought. Just in case.

He waited a half hour, and was about to give up, when the door opened and she came out. She was dressed now in sneakers, a pair of jeans, and a dark sweater and windbreaker.

At the curb, she turned right and took off at a brisk pace.

Carter followed, keeping in shadows and darting through the pools of light coming from the infrequent streetlamps.

Her pace was fast, and there was no attempt to check to see if she were being followed. Also, there was very little maneuvering.

Louise Marino had a definite destination and she was heading right for it.

The dank weather had turned into a light mist that, in turn, became swirling fog as they approached the lake. Carter welcomed it and shortened the distance between them.

At the westernmost edge of Tegel Forest, Louise turned in to a small cemetery. He gave her a little more distance and then followed her up the cobbled walk.

Suddenly Carter heard voices.

A man: "You got rid of him early."

Louise: "He's a boorish lout. He tried to seduce me."

A laugh.

Carter moved forward, staying in the silence of the grass until he spotted them standing by an army-issue dark green sedan.

The man was very tall, a couple of inches taller than Carter, with a hawkish face, a strong chin, and deep blue eyes behind horn-rimmed glasses. His hair was jet black with gray at the temples that matched his damp suit.

"I can't say as I blame him for trying to get you into bed, Louise."

The man stepped forward as though to take her in his arms. Just as his hands touched her shoulders, Louise flattened her own hands on his chest and shoved him with all her strength against the sedan.

"That's over, remember?" she murmured.

"All right, all right, take it easy."

"No, *you* take it easy," she retorted. "Now, let's get with it. Cemeteries give me the creeps. I don't know why I couldn't just telephone you."

"Because he might have had your phone tapped. Besides, cemeteries are very peaceful and quiet. You can hear someone approach from ten crypts away."

Carter looked around. The man was right. There was no way he could get any closer to the car.

"Get in the car," the man continued, taking Louise's arm and guiding her into the sedan. "I have the tape recorder ready. I want to hear every word he said."

Carter cursed, but he knew it was a dead end. The windows were up in the car and it was in the middle of a small traffic circle.

But at least he had a face.

He turned up his collar and retraced his steps back to the gates. Three blocks farther on, he hailed a cab and directed the driver to the base.

In his rooms at the bachelor officers' quarters, he stripped and took a warm shower. Then, with a towel around his middle and a brandy at his side, he removed a small leather-bound case from the false bottom of his suitcase.

The case was no larger than a cigar box. Inside was a small projector for microfilm. He took the microfilm from the chrome cylinder. There were fourteen microslides: seven dossiers, seven pictures.

Quickly, he went through the personnel files, matching each one with a face and memorizing the whole.

He hit the jackpot on the next-to-last set:

FOX, RANDOLPH JOHN, COLONEL USA-R.
SERIAL NUMBER 481945692
BORN: NEW YORK CITY 4-18-48
COMMISSIONED: 9-20-70

Carter looked at the man's promotion history; it hadn't taken him many years to make full bird colonel. The Killmaster made a mental note. Fox was either a very bright guy or he had good friends.

He skipped over education, commendations, and family background to current status:

HEAD OF INTELLIGENCE LIAISON BE-
TWEEN U.S. ARMY, WEST BERLIN, AND
BUNDESAMT fur VERFASSUNGSSCHUTZ
(BfV).

Carter digested the whole file as he had the others, then sat back and took a sip of his brandy.

"Well, well, well," he said aloud.

Colonel Randolph John Fox and Lieutenant Louise Marino's midnight man were one and the same.

FOUR

Commander Howard Knapp gave the backpack boosters a quick surge and glided through the shuttle's hatch into dark space. He moved unerringly, with his white umbilical cord trailing behind him toward G.P.S. 12.

"Cleared the hatch . . . moving out," Knapp said.

"Check, Howard, you're off two degrees to starboard, approximately ninety yards below."

The voice echoing in his helmet belonged to Mildred Lessing, communications coordinator for this shuttle flight.

Knapp made the adjustment and searched the blackness before him. "Got it—homing in."

What Knapp "got" was a sighting on one of NAVSTAR's eighteen satellites that made up the Global Positioning Tracking System—Number 12, to be exact.

Because of an apparent malfunction in the satellite's guidance system, it had slewed out of its orbit in the geostationary belt.

"Contact."

"Check."

Using his hands delicately on the specified areas around the satellite's myriad antennae, Knapp pulled himself toward the belly of the beast.

Three levers opened the faceplate that covered the satellite's brain. Two tiny lights on his helmet illumined the four circuit boards inside.

"Negative on a visual check. Everything looks okay."

"Hook up. We'll monitor and checklist in here."

"Right."

It took Knapp ten minutes to pull clips and wires from the utility belt around his waist and begin the series of twenty-four attachments necessary. The other end of the wires ran inside his suit and through the umbilical cord to the master computer inside the shuttle.

"Ready."

"Beginning check," Lessing replied.

It was out of Knapp's hands now. The shuttle's master computer would detect the malfunction and inform them what must be done to repair it.

Knapp dropped his gaze from the side of the satellite and glanced from the twinkling lights in the silent blackness to the familiar blue marble called Earth.

"Hi, Mom."

"What?"

"Nothing."

The readout took eight minutes.

"We have surges in one of the power cables."

"Right."

Knapp unhooked himself and moved around the satellite to a second plate. As he revolved the levers to unhinge it, the lights on his helmet fell across the skin and made him pause.

"That's odd . . ."

"What is it?" Lessing asked.

"The skin on the power plate—it's seared."

"You mean burned?"

"Yeah."

"Any dents?—A meteor, maybe?"

"Negative," Knapp replied. "It's more like the run of a blowtorch."

"Did it pierce the skin?"

"No, but it looks like it got hotter than hell."

"Check the cables, then photograph the skin when you close it back up."

"Right."

Knapp found the same evidence of heat and searing on the inner side of the plate.

"Cable Two is soft. Looks and feels as though it's the result of severe heat."

"Can it be spliced?"

"Check, will do."

A half hour later Knapp was back on the shuttle with G.P.S. 12 functioning properly again. The helmet was barely lifted from his head before one of his fellow crew members withdrew its miniature camera.

"They want these photos downstairs pronto, Howard. Also, a detailed visual report from you."

"Roger."

Mildred Lessing was the first to see the photos before they were sent back to earth. A great deal of her training had been in the research of light amplification by stimulated emission of radiation.

Mildred Lessing knew a laser beam when she saw one.

Within three hours, her superiors at NASA had come to the same conclusion.

There were twenty men in the room, a mixture of space and intelligence groups as well as representatives from the Pentagon.

Dr. Michael Hamm, director of Argon Research Laboratories, specializing in lasers, had the floor.

"For quite some time, both we and the Soviet Union have been trying to perfect a satellite-borne laser system that would be capable of destroying other satellites and missiles. Until now, it wasn't feasible."

"Why not, Dr. Hamm?"

"Because the means of focusing the laser or particle

beam was inadequate to create the desired amount of damage . . . in other words, to fry the innards of a satellite or missile.''

"Doctor . . .?''

"Yes . . . uh . . .''

"Hawk, David Hawk . . . Intelligence. Does the evidence from G.P.S. Twelve bring you to believe that the Soviets have perfected such a beam?''

Hamm removed his glasses, rubbed his eyes, and replied without replacing them.

"No. But I would say, Mr. Hawk, that they are damned close.''

"Closer than we are?''

"One hell of a lot closer.''

David Hawk exchanged a worried glance with his CIA counterpart and eased his stocky body back into his chair.

For the next hour he worked an unlit cigar to shreds as he listened to the scientists explain what could be the consequences of this new Soviet technology.

By the end of that time, he had heard the principles of chemical and X-ray lasers, Excimer lasers, and what most of them could do if they were positioned in space and with a powerful enough beam.

David Hawk cared little for the technological aspects of what he heard. It was the result that struck him.

"If there are no further questions, gentlemen . . .''

"One question, Doctor.''

"Yes, Mr. Hawk?''

"From scientific journals, conventions, or any other means, have you the names of Soviet or Eastern bloc scientists who might be foremost in perfecting this type of laser and the satellite to beam it?''

Hamm did his glasses routine a second time, and slowly recited three names.

Hawk made a mental note of the names, then asked a last question. "Of those three, Dr. Hamm, who would, in your opinion, be most likely to make the breakthrough?''

"Beyond a doubt, Adolph Grinsing."

"Thank you."

A half hour later David Hawk sat across the desk from his CIA counterpart.

"I'll alert all our deep-cover people in Poland and Czechoslovakia. If it is Grinsing, they should turn up something."

Hawk nodded. *"If* Hamm's theory is correct that the beam originated in that area."

"It's all we have to go on right now. If we do come up with anything, what do you suggest?"

Hawk through for a full minute before replying.

"Send someone in, evaluate the situation, and, if the research can be nipped at the source, terminate."

The other man shrugged and sighed. "I didn't hear that, of course."

"Of course not." Hawk stood. "Keep me posted."

"Will do."

The two men shook hands, and David Hawk took the elevator to the underground garage.

"Home," he growled, settling into the rear of the waiting limousine.

The chauffeur knew that "home" didn't mean the Spartan condo that David Hawk owned. Home was the AXE offices on Dupont Circle in Washington, D.C.

The big car was barely through the gates of Langley before Hawk was on the phone to his chief assistant, Ginger Bateman.

"Get a progress report on Alderstaadt from Carter. We might need that tunnel operative sooner than we thought!"

FIVE

The first week under Colonel Carter's command was hectic but exhilarating. Wilson proved to be an excellent planner and speedy builder. Excavation had already started on the site, and all materials necessary had been requisitioned through General Wells. A delivery date had been set, and Wilson had guaranteed that site preparation would be completed by the date of their delivery.

Major Hardin was able to acquire his communications equipment in such a roundabout way that, so far, no one had suspected the real reason for the building beyond its being just another radar installation.

Carter felt that the project was running itself well enough that he could pursue the second half of his assignment: the uncovering of Copperhead.

Marty Jacobs had given him all the cooperation, and more, that Carter requested.

Twenty-four-hour surveillance teams had been assigned to all seven of the liaison members, with special attention paid to Colonel Randolph Fox.

Carter had made his peace with Louise Marino, and since the initial night of the meeting with Fox, all efforts on her part to dig any deeper into the Alderstaadt project had ceased.

A full background check had been done, and Marino had come out clean as fresh laundry. Marty Jacobs had turned up a two-year affair between her and Fox. That, Carter assumed, would explain her actions toward the colonel that night in the cemetery.

Carter guessed that she was as clean as she looked, but he had Jacobs keep tabs on her anyhow.

Twice a day the Killmaster checked in with AXE Berlin by neutral phone for evaluation reports on all of them.

By the second week a pattern emerged on Fox and one other team member: Captain Bernard Evers, a Canadian.

Evers was a protégé of Fox and answered directly to him. His main job was to assess reports on West German spooks who spied on known East German spooks operating in West Germany. In the time since Carter had arrived, Evers had shown as much interest in the Crown Prince project as his boss, Fox, had exhibited.

The Killmaster had evaluated this two ways: Evers could be snooping at Fox's command; or he could be doing it on his own and using Fox as a double cover.

Carter narrowed his own suspicions to the two men and decided to bait the hook for both of them.

"You're two hours ahead of schedule, Nick. There's nothing new."

"That's okay, Marty. I want to put some misinformation in the pipeline. Who would I talk to that would probably pass it along to Evers but has no contact with Fox?"

There was no hesitation from the other end of the line. "Franz Poulson. Real slime. He deals dope, whores, and information for both sides. The local boys haven't leaned on him because we use him ourselves every now and then."

"Where would I find him?"

"He operates a sex shop and porno theater on the Ku' Damm."

"Where do his girls work?"

"Mostly out of the small clubs around the theater. Be careful, Nick. It's a rough district."

Carter chuckled. "I've been mugged in the worst."

For the next two nights Carter caroused in the strip and jive clubs up and down the Kurfursten Damm. He alternated between making himself generally obnoxious and openly a security risk. He let it be known to strippers, B-girls, and bartenders that he was in Berlin on a very hush-hush assignment. He dropped hints about its importance, and his own.

There were no takers, and by the fifth night he was about to give up.

Then he met Fräulein Elke Zinder. She was called "Boom Boom," and one look at her proportions told him why.

It was in one of the sleazier clubs, the Cat's Meow, and she was the headliner. He was about to leave after the first show, when Boom Boom dropped her six-foot frame into the chair beside him and rested her two claims to exotic immortality on the table.

"Buy me a drink, Colonel?"

"Sure."

Unlike the special drink of the other girls—watery champagne cocktails—Boom Boom preferred whiskey, and she drank it like a longshoreman.

"You come every night. I see you. I like you."

"I like you, too," Carter slurred. "There's a lot to like. Where do you go after the orgy?"

"I have rooms at the Kinderhof . . . Number Thirty-eight."

"What time?"

"My last show is two o'clock."

"Shall we say three o'clock at Number Thirty-eight?"

"That would be nice. *Prosit.*"

Four straight whiskies later she left to get undressed for her next show.

Carter waited until the show started before staggering

from the club. It wasn't all an act; he had matched the Amazon drink for drink and was beginning to feel the effects.

Three blocks from the club he found a phone booth. He dialed and was put through to Marty Jacobs's apartment.

"Elke Zinder, they call her Boom Boom. She made the same pitch as the others but asked for no money up front. She might be a live one."

"Unless she just goes for your drunken charm," Jacobs replied with a chuckle. "What's the number where you are?"

Carter told him and hung up. Two cigarettes later he grabbed the phone when it barely jingled.

"She's one of Poulson's, and she doesn't come cheap. If she offered you a freebie, there's an ulterior motive."

"Good enough. My last known address will be Number Thirty-eight, the Kinderhof."

"I'll give you a couple of watchers."

Carter hung up and headed for a greasy spoon across the street. He wanted to fortify his stomach for the bout to come.

The Kinderhof wasn't exactly respectable, but it was several steps above a fleabag.

Number 38 was on the sixth floor, and Boom Boom answered the door herself. Carter had already seen her stark naked that night, so all the flesh that gleamed through the sheer tent she wore didn't move him.

Nevertheless, he managed an enthusiastic leer as she led him inside. In the middle of the sitting room she stopped, whirled, and gathered him to her much like a momma octopus.

"You are big," she said, kneading his buttocks and trying to spear his eardrum with her tongue.

"Boom Boom," Carter replied, rolling his chest across her namesakes, "so are you."

"You are big man in army?"

"Very big."

"You make lots of money?"

"Not enough."

"That's too bad. Boom Boom likes handsome Americans who make lots of money."

"Since I don't, is our date off?"

"We'll see," she replied with a laugh that seemed to rattle the windows. "Come, we drink, but not whiskey. We drink good German schnapps!"

She rounded up a bottle and two glasses, and joined him on the couch.

"What do you do for army?" she asked, pouring.

"I'm a spy."

"*Gut!* All Berlin is full of spies, all spying on each other. *Prosit!*"

The clear liquid took off the back of his head and then boiled its way down to his gut. The glass barely left his lips before she grabbed it and returned it, full.

A half hour later they were no closer to the bedroom, nor had Boom Boom made any pitch for her boss. And the bottle was half empty.

Through bleary eyes, the Killmaster checked the room as she prattled on about the many American friends she had known over the years. He couldn't spot the bug, but he knew it was there, somewhere close to where they sat. Twice he had started to move, and both times she had pulled him unceremoniously back down to her side.

Sensing that his interest in her monumental charms was waning, she took a few minutes out from her chatter each time to work him over.

Just about the time he thought the whole evening was bombing out, she hit him with both barrels.

"I, too, am spy, you know."

"Oh?"

"*Ja,* for East Germany. They pay very good. I save my money and soon I retire."

"I'll have you arrested." Carter laughed drunkenly.

"Why do that? I help you make money, too. Then you can show Boom Boom a good time, and Boom Boom give you a good time!"

"You're crazy."

"You think so? We'll see. C'mon, we make love now!"

She was swift, sure, and calculating. He was naked, raped, dressed, and out of the hotel in just under an hour.

At nine o'clock the next morning, Carter stumbled past Lieutenant Marino.

"You look like hell."

"I feel worse."

At ten-thirty an envelope arrived marked *Personal, Colonel N. Carter, For Your Eyes Only.*

"Who delivered this?"

Louise shrugged. "A commercial messenger service. I didn't get the name. Something wrong?"

"No. Thanks."

He waited until the door closed behind her before ripping open the envelope.

Inside were ten prints and a typewritten note.

Carter examined each of the prints and grinned to himself at the contortions the human body was capable of in the throes of lust.

The note was simple and to the point:

Colonel Carter:

If you wish the negatives to these and ten others just like them, as well as the master recording of the evening, call 445-991 Berlin at eight sharp this evening.

The note wasn't signed.

Crude, Carter thought. The Russians did it much better and much less obviously.

But then, Poulsen and Company were amateurs just trying to emulate the big boys.

He put the prints in his briefcase and headed for the door.

"I'm taking an early lunch and probably won't be back for the rest of the day."

Louise nodded as if she could care less, and Carter made for the street. He darted into the first bar he saw, nervously ordered a drink, and headed for the phone.

"Yeah, Nick, what's up?"

"I got a bingo on Elke Zinder. Are you sure she's connected only with Poulson?"

"Positive."

"Okay, I got pictures and they have a tape. It's the usual blackmail scam. I'm to call them at eight tonight."

Jacobs chuckled. "I'd love to see the pictures. I've seen Boom Boom."

Carter matched his laugh. "Actually, they're quite good. All in all, I'd say I fought her to a draw."

"Congratulations! What's next?"

"Contact General Wells. Give him a rundown on the whole thing. Also, get word to Klaus Klassen on the other side to watch out for the material. You know what to tell him to look for."

"Right."

Carter hung up and made a second call.

"Major Hardin, please."

Steve Hardin came on the line seconds later.

"Hardin here."

"Steve, Nick. Get in touch with Jim Wilson at the site. Tell him to meet you and me at the Meinsingarten for an emergency lunch."

"Jesus, Nick, they're starting the dig today. He'll be pissed . . ."

"This is an emergency. Tell him . . . one hour."

Carter gulped his drink, paid, and returned to the street. At the motor pool, he found Sergeant Barnes.

''Take me to Templehof and then take the rest of the day off.''

''Something wrong?''

''No, why?'' Carter growled.

Barnes shrugged. ''You just seem edgy.''

''Family problems,'' Carter muttered. ''Move!''

In his BOQ room, he showered and changed into civilian clothes. Just before leaving, he taped the pictures under one of the dresser drawers. The last thing he did was memorize the telephone number and burn the note.

Wilson and Hardin were waiting in a dim rear section of the restaurant when Carter arrived. Wisely, they had chosen a corner booth that stood alone, several feet from any of its neighbors.

''What the hell's up?'' Wilson demanded. ''The crew is already ten feet down and shoring. I should be there!''

''Spook stuff, shhh.''

Carter ordered a stein of lager and made chitchat until the waiter brought it and left.

''Okay, if you're ten feet down, that means you're ahead of the game.''

Wilson nodded. ''At this rate, I figure we'll hit the wall about a week early.''

''And you're set on how to get into the bunker?''

''If the info you gave me is correct.''

''It is,'' Carter said, and turned to Steve Hardin. ''How are you set?''

''Gangbusters. I've got the circuitry down pat, and I've laid out a cable system. With the equipment description you got me from the other side, the match should be perfect. They'll never know we were in there.''

''Good,'' Carter sighed, and sipped his beer. ''It looks like everything's going according to the clock. And that's important, because from now on until completion, you might have to run the whole project.''

"Why?" Wilson asked.

"Because I've been a bad boy and I may have to go to jail for a while."

"What?" both men exclaimed in unison.

"It's a tricky business, but here's the gist of it."

Quickly Carter explained the presence of Copperhead, and the importance both for Crown Prince specifically and West German intelligence in general that the man be exposed.

"But why the can for you?" Wilson asked.

"That's not for sure," Carter replied. "It's just a guess. But if it does happen, I want to know that the two of you can finish the project on your own."

The two men exchanged looks, then nodded as one.

"Sure, no problem."

"But what about my three-man comm team when the time comes?" Hardin asked.

"They're set and ready to roll when you need them." Carter slipped a box of matches across the table. "Memorize the number I've written on the inside of that, then burn it. You'll be talking to an agent named Marty Jacobs. He's good, and he can get you anything you want. Everything clear?"

"Sure."

"How much time will you have to do, Nick?"

Carter chuckled. "Not more than a few days, I hope."

"What's the charge gonna be?"

Here Carter laughed aloud. "Probably indecent exposure."

SIX

The Killmaster spent the remainder of the afternoon and early evening working his way toward the Kinderhof and along the Kurfursten Damm, bar by bar.

Anyone coming in contact with him saw alternately a man consumed by anger and what appeared to be frustration and humiliation.

By the time he reached the door of the Cat's Meow, he was also a man who appeared roaring drunk.

Other than the bartender, two customers, and a beefy bouncer playing solitaire at the end of the bar, the place was empty.

"*Ja, mein Herr?*"

"I want to see Elke Zinder," Carter growled in English.

"Der girls don't come in until nine."

"Where are the dressing rooms?"

The bartender started to raise his arm from instinct to point toward the rear. At the last second, however, he thought better of it and shook his head.

"Fräulein Zinder doesn't work here anymore."

"Bullshit," Carter hissed, moving down the bar.

He was nearly to the end when the big bouncer moved off his stool to block Carter's way.

"No one in the back."

"I'll see for myself."

Their eyes met and held.

Carter relaxed, letting his body and mind do a yoga exercise that brought a mantle of coldness down across his face.

The other man saw it and paused for a second. It was a second too long.

Carter kicked him hard in the right kneecap, spinning him around. Then the Killmaster grabbed him by the back of the belt and smashed him, headfirst, into the wall. The giant's butt made a thudding sound hitting the floor. He was still awake, but woozy.

Carter didn't give him time to recover higher than his good knee. He plowed the toe of a size nine into his gut and pulled him forward by the hair. At the same time, he curled his right hand around the man's face and smashed the back of his head twice against the wall.

This time he went down to stay.

The sound of clomping feet on the hardwood floor spun the Killmaster around.

The two at the table evidently were more than just customers. They were coming for him side by side, frantically clawing at their belts for a couple of small-caliber handguns.

Carter tensed the muscle in his right forearm, releasing a pencil-thin stiletto he affectionately called Hugo into his hand.

He surprised both of them by standing his ground and meeting them head-on.

Carter shouldered one of them in the gut, sending him sprawling back over a table. The other caught the stiletto clear through his forearm above the gun hand. The man screamed, and the little revolver clattered to the floor. Carter kicked it away, and ruined the man's sex life for a few months with a well-aimed kick in the groin.

Number One was staggering to his feet, searching the floor for his gun with glazed eyes.

Carter calmly flipped a table and smashed it down over the man's head.

"That's enough!"

Carter turned. The barman had moved out. He stood now in front of the bar, his hands holding the gun Carter had kicked away. The muzzle was swaying about six inches from side to side, telling the Killmaster that the man wasn't too sure he could back up his words.

"Stay right there . . . don't move!"

"Think you've got the guts?" Carter said, advancing step by step, daring the man with slitted eyes and fists swaying at the end of his arms. "Better kill me on the first shot, bastard."

"I won't kill you, swine. I'll just gut-shoot you and watch you bleed."

Big words, but by the time the nervous gun fired, Carter was already too close and dived under the slug.

He shouldered the gun to the side before a second shot could be fired, and filled the man's belly with his right fist.

The gun fell to the floor. Carter gave him a fast right, then a knee in the gut that straightened him up against the bar. Then he measured him and mashed his beetlike nose all over his face. Carter was setting up for another, when he saw the eruption coming.

The Killmaster stepped aside just before the vomit flew. When the puddle on the floor was ample, he dropped its creator into it.

In the dressing room, a lone young woman in a frumpy maid's costume huddled against a series of lockers behind an ironing board.

"Get out."

She nodded and ran fast.

Carter had already made his plans. It took him exactly

fifteen minutes to methodically trash the dressing rooms.
The ripped gowns and shattered mirrors and spilled jars of
cosmetics would all point to a man at the end of his rope.

And the mess he had made of the hoods in the bar would
tell them how irrationally dangerous he could be.

The goons were still sound asleep in their own blood
when he left, locking the door behind him.

At a flower shop across from the Kinderhof, he bought
a dozen white carnations.

In the Kinderhof, he took the stairs three at a time and
stopped in front of Number 38.

"*Ja?*"

"Fräulein Zinder?"

"*Ja?*"

"Flowers, Fräulein. A bouquet for you."

The chain fell, the lock tumbler rolled, the door opened,
and Boom Boom barely had time to remark on the
bouquet's beauty before it was in her face.

Carter came in right behind the flowers, slamming the
door behind him and locking it.

"You . . . !"

"Me . . . good night, Boom Boom."

There was more accuracy than strength in the blow. It
landed on the very point of her chin, and she landed with a
very loud thud on the floor.

Carter performed the same miracle on the two rooms of
Boom Boom's apartment that he had previously executed
on the Cat's Meow dressing rooms. He paid special attention to her wardrobe, piling each gown on top of the other
after shredding it.

Carter spent the hour between seven and eight urging a
foot-paddle boat around the Tegeler See. He was fairly
sure they had picked him up at some point that afternoon.
If they had, and they were watching him now, their image
of an angry, frustrated, and confused man would be more
than complete.

At precisely eight, he docked the boat, got his deposit for its safe return, and made for the telephone on the boathouse wall.

"*Ja?*" came the voice on the first ring.

"This is Carter."

"You are a madman."

"Now that you know what I am, who and what are you?"

"We merely wanted a few pieces of information, but your stupid revenge has made it more difficult."

"That's a pity. Where do I meet you? I am now at—"

"We know where you are. Take the U-Bahn to Rathaus Neukolln. At ten sharp, the steamer *Moby Dick* stops there on its return trip up the Havel."

"I know of it."

"Good. There is one stop at Strandbad before the end of the ride at the Tegel Airport jetty. Get off at Strandbad and go into the *Biergarten* above the pool. Do you understand that?"

"Yes. Then what?"

"You will be contacted."

The line went dead, and Carter crossed the street to the U-Bahn.

They were cutting it thin. He had only three minutes to purchase a ticket and board the steamer. In the bar, he sucked at a beer and tried to make his tail.

They were good. For the next forty-five minutes, Carter had the unmistakable chill up his spine that he was being carefully watched, but he couldn't spot the watcher.

At Strandbad he followed instructions and climbed the two flights of steps leading to the open air *Biergarten* above the huge pool.

In the middle of his second beer, a buxom waitress moved through the tables, calling his name.

"Here, Fräulein."

"Herr Carter?"

"*Ja.*"

"You have a call, mein Herr. There, near the pool door."

"*Danke.*"

He shoved a bill into her hand and made for the phone.

"Very wise, Colonel. You have no one following you."

"Except you. What now?" Carter kept the belligerence in his tone, but also the frustration. Eventually he would fold before this man, but he couldn't let it happen too easily.

"Walk two blocks away from the river, turn right to Jagrowstrasse, and wait there on the corner."

Again the phone went dead in his ear.

The section around the pool was a mixture of middle-class residential and small shops, most of them connected in some way with the traffic on the river.

A half block short of Jagrowstrasse, a black Mercedes sedan slid to a halt beside him and the rear door opened.

"Get in!"

Carter was scarcely in the seat before the car lurched forward, closing the door with its motion.

There were three of them, two in front and one beside him. The one beside him looked like a member of Hitler Youth all grown up: bright blue eyes, a handsome, chiseled jaw, pale blond hair, and a hefty Mauser in his left hand pointing at Carter's chest.

From Marty Jacobs's description, Carter knew it was Franz Poulson.

"Do you have a weapon?"

"No."

"You used a knife in my bar."

"A stiletto, to be exact," Carter replied. "And I left it home. Who are you?"

Poulson passed the Mauser to the front-seat passenger, who leveled it on Carter. Then the blond man leaned back and took his time lighting a small cigar.

"It is not important that you know my name. You take a very good picture."

"How much?" Carter asked, nervously cracking his knuckles.

"Fifty thousand American."

"You're nuts."

Poulson shrugged and blew a stream of smoke toward Carter's face. "It is my price. I have a great deal of overhead."

"I don't have a snowball's chance in hell of coming up with fifty thousand dollars."

"Those pictures of you fornicating with a known East German agent would ruin your career, Herr Colonel."

Carter shrugged. "I doubt that. Maybe I'd be put behind a desk in some backwater, but not much else."

Poulson smiled. "True, perhaps, but this . . ."

He leaned forward and opened a panel in the back of the front seat. Inside was a mini-bar and a tape deck. A switch was flicked, and the interior of the sedan filled with Carter's and Elke Zinder's voices.

As the tape played through, Carter forced the color from his face and went about cracking his knuckles even more nervously.

Inside, he was telling himself that Poulson and Company were more than the amateurs he had previously considered them to be.

The tape was a product of extremely clever editing, and Elke Zinder had followed a master script in her chattering questions that, at the time, he had thought inane.

The finished conversation sounded as though Carter had totally committed himself to doing business with the woman.

"Well?" Poulson said, turning off the machine.

"I'd be indicted for treason."

"Most assuredly. There is no way you can meet my price?"

"None, I swear it," Carter said, wringing his hands and sweating now. "I could raise . . . maybe twenty."

"Not enough. But perhaps there is another way . . ."

"How? I'll do anything."

"This radar installation you're building . . ."

"No."

"It is not a radar installation. There are three such installations already in West Berlin, more than enough to give your government the intelligence you need."

"It *is* a radar installation," Carter insisted.

"It isn't. There are certain people who will pay me for this information. Once I receive that payment, you shall receive the negatives and the tape."

"Go to hell!"

"Suit yourself. Stop the car."

The Mercedes came to a halt, but Carter sat, sweating. He took just long enough to convince Poulson of his inner torment before he spoke again.

"What do you want to know?" he sighed at last.

Again Poulson leaned forward. He changed the cassette tape in the deck and turned it on again, this time to Record.

"Shall we begin?"

"It's a combination intercept and jamming terminal. We know the East Germans are renovating a bunker in Alderstaadt as a communications terminus. We have developed a new sensor that can intercept signals directly from electrical impulses . . ."

"Yes . . . go on."

"The electric feed into the bunker is overhead. The sensor we have developed, when trained on those feed lines, can detect the signals."

Poulson practically rubbed his hands together. "I want the specifications of this sensor, all of them!"

"I don't have them. I mean, I don't have them in my head."

"But you can get them."

Again Carter hesitated. "Yes . . . I can."

"Call the same number tomorrow night at eight sharp. Stop the car here!"

The Mercedes slid to the curb. Poulson leaned across Carter and pushed the door open.

"Walk across the bridge, there. You'll find a taxi stand. Eight o'clock tomorrow evening, Colonel, sharp."

It took all of Carter's will not to walk across the bridge with a light, springing step.

The play was in motion.

With any luck, by six o'clock in the morning the East Germans would be running a new underground cable into the bunker, and Copperhead would be hungry for his second tidbit!

As he did at the end of every workday, no matter how late the hour, Captain Bernard Evers hand-carried his daily report into Colonel Fox's office.

Fox was still at his desk.

"Bernie."

"Colonel," Evers replied, dropping the folder on his superior's desk. "Another day of quiet on the Eastern front."

Fox scanned the report quickly. It contained bits and pieces of information on the movements of known East German agents in the West, as well as minor reports from West German tipsters who made extra money watching possible agents.

"Nothing on this Carter or his project?"

"No, sir," Evers replied, lighting a small cigar. "I've alerted several of our people, but so far nothing."

"Damn!" Fox growled. "I'm supposed to keep the West Germans informed of what we're doing, and my own people don't even keep *me* informed."

"It is a touchy situation, Colonel, I agree. They shouldn't go over your head."

"You're damned right they shouldn't! Christ, I'm liaison! How can I clear something if I don't even know what it is?"

Evers smiled around his cigar, hiding it with his cupped hand. Colonel Randy Fox had an ego as big as all outdoors. Anything that didn't pass over his desk that he considered he should know about rattled that ego.

Evers had used that trait in the other man several times in the past to his advantage.

"Anything from General Wells or Lieutenant Marino?"

"The general told me to buzz off, keep my nose out of it. Can you imagine that, Bernie? . . . buzz off? Jesus, they could put ten snoops on that project and I couldn't even warn them!"

"I agree, sir. It's hard to pass on intelligence if you don't know what you're looking for."

"Damned right. And Louise won't give me the time of day. She practically told me to buzz off as well. Says Carter doesn't tell her a thing."

"I'll keep on it, sir. By the way, we have a clearance request on ten men from Spandgarten."

Evers dropped a list of each, with a security clearance form, in front of Fox.

"You've checked them all?"

"Yes, sir. All clean as a whistle."

"Any idea what they're to be used for?"

"No, sir. It was a blind request. If you'll initial them, I'll get them across town by messenger this evening."

Fox grunted and scrawled his initials on the ten forms. It was a common thing. He always left clearance checks up to Evers. It was a boring procedure and Fox couldn't be bothered with it.

Evers held his breath until all ten forms were initialed, and then he held it a few seconds longer.

But everything was fine. As usual, Fox didn't leaf

through the request. If he had, he would have discovered that Evers had lied. The file did contain the reason for the ten men's clearance requests, as well as their specialty.

They were to be employed for approximately three weeks, and all ten of them were miners.

"Thank you, sir. Anything else?"

"No, Bernie, it's late—time both of us got out of here."

"Yes, sir."

Captain Bernard Evers returned to his office one floor below. He made copies of the entire clearance brief, filed the copies, and sealed the originals in a large manila envelope.

At the night-duty desk, he passed the envelope over to the duty officer.

"See that this gets out with the ten o'clock messenger service."

"Sure thing, Captain. Good night."

"Good night."

As he did every night, Bernard Evers stopped in at a bar three blocks from his offices. He barely hit the door when a small glass of schnapps and a small stein of lager were set up on the bar.

"Evening, Herr Evers."

"Herr Kroger," he nodded, saluting the barman and downing the schnapps. He took a sip of the beer and moved to a bank of phones in the rear of the bar.

He had already memorized the number from Herman Bachman's request for security clearance.

"*Ja?*"

"Bachman?"

"*Ja.*"

"Copperhead."

"*Ja, mein Herr.*" The vocal tone changed to instant alertness at the mention of Evers's code name.

"You are cleared, Herr Bachman. I will want daily

reports on the project as soon as you begin."

"Ja, mein Herr. The usual method of delivery?"

"Yes. Success, Herr Bachman."

"Danke, mein Herr."

Evers hung up and moved to the washroom. He used the urinal and then carefully washed his hands. After drying them at the towel roll, he took a small key from his pocket and opened the towel container.

Deftly, he worked his fingers behind the roll and extracted an envelope. Slipping the envelope into his pocket, he relocked the container and returned to the bar. Two long swallows and the remainder of his beer was gone.

"Good night, Kroger."

"Danke, mein Herr."

At the corner kiosk he bought copies of *The International Herald-Tribune* and *Der Zeitung*. Over his shoulder he spotted the tail that had been on him for the last six days.

Evers had already photographed the man and run him through all the searches, including East Berlin. The search had come up nil, no affiliation.

At first that had bothered Evers. But then he had discovered that all his coworkers, including Fox and Lieutenant Louise Marino, had also acquired watchers.

Some agency apparently had suspicions, but since they were obviously fishing, Evers had reasoned that he was in no danger.

He reached St. Mark's Square and entered a small restaurant across from the cathedral.

"Guten Abend, Herr Evers."

"Good evening, Herr Balsom."

"Table for one, mein Herr?"

"Yes, please."

The question was superfluous. Evers ate in the same place every evening, and he always ate alone.

Over brandy and coffee he glanced through most of the *Tribune* before scanning the personal ads.

It was there.

Come ye after me, and I will make you to become fishers of men (Mark 1:17).

He folded the *Tribune* and opened *Der Zeitung*.

The same biblical citation was there.

"Will there be anything else, mein Herr?"

"No, no. As usual, everything was delicious," Evers replied, dropping bills on the table and rising.

"Danke, mein Herr."

Evers crossed the street and entered the cathedral. He dipped his fingers into the font, crossed himself, and moved up the side aisle toward the confessionals.

Only one was in use. There were four souls in the pew across from it, waiting. The old crone, all in black, was second in line.

Evers moved into the pew and bowed his head in prayer. His lips moved in silent worship, but they smiled at the same time; Bernhard Haupson's faith rested elsewhere.

At the age of ten he had been recruited into the Young Communist League. At the age of sixteen, after intensive training in East Germany, which included acquiring a command of English that was virtually accentless, he had immigrated to Vancouver, Canada. There he had been given new identity papers under the name of Bernard Evers and was sent to Toronto to live with his "aunt" and "uncle," Clarice and Homer Evers.

Both Clarice and Homer Evers had been Soviet agents all their adult lives.

At the age of twenty-one, after graduating from college, Bernard joined the Canadian Royal Air Force. He did not qualify for flight instruction, but other aptitudes took him into intelligence work.

In ten years' time, he distinguished himself and attained the rank of captain. When an opening came up as liaison between Canadian military intelligence and the American CIA, Evers was accepted. After two years in Washington, he was able to attach himself to Colonel Randolph Fox. When Fox was transferred to Berlin, he took his very valuable Canadian protégé with him.

The old woman exited the confessional. The young man beside Evers entered, and Evers himself slid to the end of the pew.

Again he prayed . . . that the solid network he had built up in West Berlin in the last year would continue to be so very profitable for the Soviet Union and the East German People's Republic.

It was his turn in the confessional.

"Forgive me, Father, for I have sinned . . ."

Evers was a viceless man, but he managed to scorch the priest's ears with sins as he groped beneath the thinly padded seat for the message the old woman had left.

His penance was ten Hail Marys and, if he so chose, a gift to the poor.

Evers dropped twenty marks into the poor box as he left the church, then walked the ten remaining blocks to his apartment.

He read the message the old woman had left first. It was from Poulson.

It was long and detailed. When he finished, Evers quickly made up a message of his own.

He checked the hall, then walked up two flights to the fifth floor. At Number 5-C he paused. The nameplate read Dr. Emil Bondorf.

Evers opened the door with a key and entered the sterile, scarcely lived-in room. He went immediately to the telephone and dialed.

"*Ja?*"

"*Herr Poulson, bitte.*"

"This is Poulson."

"I received your message, and find it quite interesting."

Colonel Randolph Fox would have been amazed to hear his trusted aide speaking such flawless German. As far as

Fox knew, Evers could not speak a word of any language other than English. In actual fact, Bernard Evers could speak four languages fluently, including Russian.

"How interesting, mein Herr?"

"The usual price, with stipulations."

"Such as?"

"I want to know your source and the means of obtaining."

"The source is a Colonel Nicholas Carter," Poulson replied, and went on to explain just how the information was obtained.

"I see. Very well, I shall pick up the diagrams of the sensor in the usual way, day after tomorrow."

"And my payment . . . ?"

"Will be on time, Herr Poulson, I assure you. Good night."

"Good night, mein Herr."

Evers broke the connection and dialed a number in Frankfurt.

"*Ja?*"

"I want to speak to Aunt Margaret. This is her nephew Emil."

"One moment."

Seconds later a woman's voice came on the line.

"*Ja, Liebchen.* How are you?"

"Fine, Aunt Margaret, just fine."

For the next twenty minutes the two of them spoke of their nonexistent families. Anyone listening to the conversation would take it for sentimental jibberish.

By the time Evers had hung up, he had relayed a report of everything that had gone through the liaison office that day, as well as a full report on what he had gleaned—and was about to glean—from Poulson.

Evers knew that within minutes a lorry driver would be dispatched from Frankfurt to the frontier with every word he had said.

From a nearby table he took a decanter of brandy and

poured himself a drink. When he had lit a small cigar, he withdrew his code book from a secret drawer beneath the table.

Then, and only then, did he open the envelope his East German direct contact had left for him in the men's room of his favorite bar.

Now, Herr Carter, let's just see who the devil you are.

He opened the code book—ironically, a copy of *Mein Kampf*—found the correct page for that day, and began to transcribe.

To: COPPERHEAD
From: KGB CENTRAL, FIRST DIRECTORATE, MOSCOW
Subject: N. CARTER, AMERICAN

Re: Your Inquiry. Subject is not—repeat, is not—a colonel, nor is he affiliated with military. He is an intelligence agent with very high priority . . .

The more Evers transcribed, the more amazed he became. By the time he had read the last two lines, he was smiling broadly.

Here, he thought, was a means of even further advancement.

Subject is considered extremely dangerous and is on First Directorate terminate list. Advise caution, but if possible urge you to find means of elimination as long as your current projects are not put in jeopardy.

Evers leaned back and took a deep drag on his cigar.
Terminate.
But don't jeopardize myself.
Evers sipped his brandy and let his mind roam.

Could it be possible that a dolt like Poulson could have actually outsmarted Carter?

Evers doubted it, but then Paulson was only a dolt in his—Evers's—eyes. Actually, the man had pulled off several intelligence coups in the past.

The supposed radar station did fall under an intelligence directive. It would stand to reason that Carter would head up its operation.

But did it stand to reason that he would let himself fall so easily into such a trap?

The information might be false. But even if it were, it made little difference. Evers would have the truth in a few days' time from the miner, Bachman.

No, it would be better to go ahead and relay the information, true or false.

Besides, he mused, if it *was* bait, he—Copperhead—would use it to upend Carter himself.

He reached for the phone.

"Poulson?"

"*Ja.*"

"There will be a large bonus in this for you. After you obtain the information from Carter, I want the Zinder woman to deliver the tape and photographs. There is a vacant house in Gatow, on the river. Have the woman come there early and bring the tape and negatives. You will direct Carter . . ."

Across the street from Evers's flat, John Byram slouched in disgust in a doorway. It was going to be a long, boring night, just like the others he had spent in the same doorway for Marty Jacobs, his boss at Berlin AXE.

Captain Bernard Evers, in Byram's opinion, was a mouse. He did the same thing every day, and never varied. If Evers was a spy, he was a damned lazy one.

Byram flipped open his notebook and made his hourly entry:

10:00 P.M. Subject tucked in bed. Lights out. Can see front and rear door of house. No one entered, no one left.

The ringing phone brought Carter from a deep sleep to instant alertness. As he reached for the receiver he checked the time. It was four in the morning.

"Yeah, Carter here."

"Marty Jacobs, Nick."

"I'll get a robe on and hit—"

"Don't bother—we're on scrambler."

"What is it?"

"Copperhead moved. We just got word from the other side."

"Klaus Klassen?"

"Yeah. They sent a team out to Alderstaadt to run a new cable to the bunker . . . underground and heavily lead insulated."

"Good enough. And . . . ?"

"And, I'm afraid, bad news."

"How so?"

"Nothing out of either Fox or Evers, not a damned thing. They both did their usual thing, no contact, no different moves, nothing."

"And the phone taps?"

"Nothing, not even anything that could be construed as code. Fox and Evers didn't even use their phones all night."

"And the others?"

"Same thing. Lieutenant Marino was the only one who even left her apartment. She went to the opera, and we had people on both sides all night long. She didn't even go to the john."

Carter sighed and lit a cigarette with his free hand.

"Okay, Marty, you did your best. Maybe we'll hit pay dirt tomorrow night."

"Let's hope so. Call me around noon."

"Will do."

Carter dropped the receiver back to its cradle and leaned back in the bed.

He inhaled deeply on the cigarette, then let the smoke seep slowly from his nostrils to spiral upward toward the ceiling.

Fox, Evers, Marino . . . all three of them checked out clean. So did the others.

Could his logic have been so wrong about Evers and Fox?

Or was Trena Klassen's information wrong?

Was Copperhead not a member of the liaison team at all?

The thought that he might have to start all over again, and this time totally in the dark, kept Carter's eyes open and his mind churning for the rest of the night.

SEVEN

Steve Hardin screwed his face into a mask of puzzlement and slurped from the coffee mug in his hand. "Yeah, Nick, I can do it, but it sounds crazy."

"Just make it sound believable. And I'll need drawings as well."

Suddenly Hardin laughed. "It might be kind of fun at that. A supersensitive Flash Gordon sensor!"

"Can I have it by eight tonight?"

"Jesus."

"It's important."

"Okay, I'll get a couple of draftsmen right on it."

"Good, but tell 'em it's a comic book for your kid or something."

"Will do.'''

Hardin was scarcely out the door when Louise Marino buzzed Carter on the intercom.

"Yeah?"

"General Wells wants to see you."

"When?"

"Ten minutes ago."

"I'll call him."

"I wouldn't. He sounds mean and mad and says for you to hop to it. His office on the double."

"You get any inkling of what it's about?"

"Not me. I don't know nothin', remember?"

Carter locked his briefcase and darted out the back way. He paused long enough in the garage to call Marty Jacobs.

"Anything?"

"Not a damned thing except on the other side. You've got 'em jumping. That underground cable is almost laid. Oh, and another tidbit from Klaus: the bunker goes on line next week."

"Next week? That's two weeks early."

"You know German efficiency."

"I'll see if I can push Major Wilson a little harder. Talk to you."

"Later. Nick, wait a minute . . ."

"Yeah?"

"Just got a message up from the code room. The man wants you."

"The man . . . you mean Hawk?"

"Yeah, he'll be in Frankfurt this afternoon. It's important."

"Damn," Carter growled. "Can you get me a ride?"

"Sure thing. Call me back in an hour."

Carter hung up and climbed into the back of the issue sedan.

"Where to, sir?"

"General Wells wants me, Sergeant. And step on it."

"Righto."

Barnes took Carter at his word and moved through Berlin traffic like it was a silent Sunday.

Twenty minutes later Carter was okayed into the general's office.

Once glance told the Killmaster something was very, very wrong. The old man's face looked like the leading edge of a thundercloud.

"General, you sent for me?"

"You bet your ass I did! What the hell is this?"

Carter was barely seated in the chair before a stapled file folder landed in his lap.

He flipped it open and read. It was a police report detailing everything he had done at Boom Boom's flat the previous afternoon.

"She went to the hospital with a fractured jaw . . . and she named you!"

Carter checked the date and time. "She took her time about it. I popped her and trashed her apartment around three yesterday afternoon. It says here that she reported it at ten this morning."

"Jesus, Carter, you mean you actually did it?"

Carter shrugged. "Part of the job, General."

The Killmaster's mind was moving. Why had Boom Boom reported all this to the police? Better yet, why would Poulson *let* her?

"So far, the lady isn't going to press charges and we've been able to squelch that report. Can you tell me why in hell you had to punch out some broad?—Worse yet, a German national?"

"You'll just have to believe me, General; it's part of the operation. Did you get any hint why she named me?"

"She didn't. According to the police inspector who filed that, her boyfriend did. When he found her, he made her tell him who did it."

Carter chuckled. "General, to be this lady's boyfriend you'd have to stand in line. I think Marty Jacobs clued you in to the fact that I might have some problems."

"Yeah," Wells hissed, "but not this kind."

"True," Carter replied, forcing himself to keep his gut feelings in his gut and his face calm, "but I didn't foresee this."

General Harley Wells's face got a little redder and his

eyes rounded in shock. "You mean there's going to be more?"

"Maybe, General. Maybe a lot more."

Herman Bachman gave his name to the khaki-clad young MP and waited stoically for his name to be found on the list.

Bachman was a hulk of a man. He had a big solid body with a short neck, a brutal, low-browed face with a simian forehead and small eyes.

Only after reading his work record and qualifications would anyone realize that Herman Bachman was an accredited engineer. He was an expert on the stress of mass per square foot as found in earth and rock.

For that reason he had been employed in mines all over Europe and England for years as a construction foreman. Always, during those terms of employment, he had supplied his East German and Soviet masters vital details about the projects he ran.

Not once in the fifteen years he had served as a spy for the East had Herman Bachman ever been suspected.

"Building Three, right down there and to the left."

"*Danke.*"

Bachman picked up his bag and moved away, his bulk and thick legs giving him a rolling gait not unlike a shipboard sailor.

Building 3 was a relic of the early postwar years, its base a Quonset hut that over a period of time had been added to and spruced up.

"Your name, please."

She was a pretty little brunette, barely out of her teens, with a corporal's insignia on the arm of her well-filled uniform.

"Bachman. Herman Bachman."

The dark head bent over a list and then came up with a smile. "Yes, right down that hall to the end. Give this number to the guard."

Bachman did as he was told and entered the large main room of the building. There were folding chairs arranged in a semicircle before a podium. All but two of the chairs were occupied.

Bachman exchanged muted greetings with two men that he had worked with before, and sat in one of the chairs.

None of the other men spoke to him. But they all knew him, mostly by reputation. Bachman was an iron-fisted taskmaster, and a loner. He also had a wild temper when provoked, and legend had it that practically anything could provoke him.

"Good morning, gentlemen. I am Major James Wilson, head of construction on this project."

There were mumbled greetings from most of the men, and Wilson moved forward to hand each of them two slips of paper and a pen.

"The first sheet is your pay rate, pension allowances, and insurance guarantees. Since all of you have worked for the U.S. military before, and on top-security projects, I'm sure you're familiar with the regulations. But read them anyway, and sign the insurance form and the security oath."

Bachman barely glanced at the papers and scrawled his signature on both of them.

"We'll be working in shifts around the clock with three-man teams and an overall foreman. Where is Bachman?"

"Here, sir."

"You'll be overall head of the teams, Bachman, and be in constant communication with me."

"Yes, sir."

"Now," Wilson said, leaning toward them over the podium, "as I mentioned, you've all worked top-security projects before, but I'm afraid nothing like this one. We hope the job will take three weeks, a month at the most. During that time you'll be sequestered here at the base.

You'll not be allowed to speak to any other personnel, civilian or military. If you accept this, you'll be taken from here to your quarters and first shift will start this afternoon. Any objections?''

There were a few grumbles and growls about not being able to see wives or girl friends—or women in general— but no one openly objected.

Bachman raised his hand. "Major?''

"Yes, Herr Bachman.''

"What about confession and mass? I am a very religious man. I pray daily at St. Mark's.''

"Sorry, it can't be allowed. However, a priest from here on the base will be available for confession and to hold a small mass for those of you who wish to attend.''

Bachman scowled but shrugged his agreement.

"Any other questions?''

A small, good-looking young man who looked more Italian than German stood with a broad grin on his face.

"Major?''

"Yes, uh . . . Burkholtz?''

"You couldn't happen to get a top-security clearance for a couple of whores, could you?''

Wilson and the others, except for Bachman, laughed heartily.

"I'll work on it, Burkholtz. Let's go.''

The men filed from the room with Bachman at their head.

He was always dour, so none of the others gave his trancelike state much thought.

He was trying to figure out an alternate way of getting his reports to Copperhead. They hadn't figured on this business of total sequestering.

The small jet landed at Frankfurt's Rhine-Main Airport and taxied to a small hangar far from the main building complex.

Carter, in civilian clothes, was down the ramp the instant it hit the deck. It was twenty paces to an unmarked black Mercedes sedan. Two overcoated men sat in the front seat. They didn't even turn around as Carter slid into the rear.

The car surged forward the second the rear door slammed, and arced around the hangar. A civilian guard held open a gate in the airport security fence and shut it the moment the Mercedes shot through.

When the car turned north toward the autobahn and the Hesse region, Carter spoke. "Marburg?"

The driver nodded and passed a folder over his shoulder to the Killmaster. It was sealed and marked *Top Secret*.

"Old man says for you to look this over . . . save time when we get there."

It was an hour's drive from Frankfurt to the charming old town of Marburg. By the time they drove through a huge wrought-iron gate and up to the door of a small schloss Axe rented as a safe house, Carter had given himself a mini-crash course in particle- and chemical-beam lasers.

David Hawk waited for him in the first-floor great room. The head of AXE paced in front of a roaring fire, a cigar in one hand, a drink in the other.

"Glad you could make it so fast, Nick."

"Yes, sir."

Something was hot. He could feel it in his bones and hear it in his boss's voice.

"Nick Carter, Dr. Michael Hamm."

"Doctor." He took the proffered hand.

"And I think you two know each other."

Carter turned toward the window where a tall, wide-backed man with sandy-blond hair had been standing. The man turned, and Carter blinked several times in disbelief.

"Klaus Klassen, how in hell . . ."

"Hello, Nick, long time. How did I get out? Copperhead asked for an intensive report on you. I volunteered to come over and get a field report from our operatives in Bonn and Frankfurt to fill out the written report from Moscow. Needless to say, I won't find out much.''

''How are you coming on Copperhead?'' Hawk asked.

''Hopefully, we're getting close. In fact, with any luck, maybe tonight.''

''Good,'' Hawk said, snapping the smoldering cigar between his teeth. ''We have to get him more than ever now. What's the latest on Alderstaadt?''

It was Hawk's way, to get all the facts on his side before laying out the motives. Carter knew it about the man and scuttled his own impatience.

''Steve Hardin is ready to go as soon as the wall is breached. We're about a week ahead on construction. Wilson has informed me he thinks he can get the tunnel completed in three weeks.''

''We might need it sooner than that,'' Klassen said, moving toward a sideboard. ''Drink, Nick?''

''Yeah, scotch . . . a couple of rocks.''

''Doctor,'' Hawk said, dropping to one of the high-backed chairs around the fireplace.

''Did you evaluate the material on the way from the airport?'' Hamm asked Carter, digging in a briefcase.

''Yeah. I think I've got an overall picture.''

''Good. Take a look at these.''

Carter accepted a stack of blowups from Hamm and a glass from Klaus Klassen. As he went through them, Hamm explained.

''For years, both the Soviet Union and our own researchers have been experimenting with all forms of lasers to be used for offensive and defensive weapons. What you're seeing there are photos of two of our satellites.''

''Burned?''

''That's right. We think it was done by an ultrapowerful chemical-beam laser.''

"Jesus," Carter hissed, dropping the photos on the desk. "The Soviets?"

Hamm nodded. "As yet we haven't perfected a beam powerful enough to do that much damage over such a span of space."

"And the Russians have?"

"Worse," Hamm said. "We think they're on the verge of perfecting a beam that can gut our satellites and knock out our missiles in the air during a retaliatory strike."

"That means," Hawk added, "that they could perfect the perfect defensive and offensive weapon . . . to be used in tandem."

Carter shook his head and rubbed the cool glass over his temples. "I don't get it."

"I'll try to explain with a supposition," Hamm said, unfolding a map of Western Europe. "Let us suppose the Soviets are toying with the idea of gobbling up industrial Europe. Okay, they invade through Poland, Czechoslovakia, and Hungary with infantry and armor, with, of course, a nuclear threat backup."

"That they don't want to use, of course," Hawk interjected.

"Exactly." Here, Hamm faced Carter directly. "If they knock out all of our surveillance satellites with lasers at the beginning of the strike, it would be hours before we could properly mobilize. By that time, they would be practically at the Rhine."

Carter sighed. "And we would have to go to missiles to stop them."

"But," Hamm said, "they would knock out our missiles in the air with their lasers. By the time we were able to fall back and reorganize to mount a ground counteroffensive, the Soviets would be at the Rhine. My guess is they would then call for a cease-fire and negotiations. Why not? They would have what they want."

Carter stifled his amazement and anger by lighting a

cigarette. "And the bastards are practicing on our satellites?"

Hamm nodded. "I think so. As far as our direction-finding equipment can determine from the hit at a precise arc in the satellite's orbit, the beam was directed from about here."

Carter leaned forward, his eyes glued to the professor's pointing finger. "Gorzow . . . Poland."

"Klaus?" Hawk said, rising and resuming his pacing.

"For several years, Nick, a huge installation has been under construction in the mountains north of Gorzow. Only recently have we been able to discover that it is being readied as a satellite launching station."

Hamm jumped in. "From that information—and the beam's direction—we have developed a theory. No matter how powerful the laser beam, it cannot follow the arc of the globe . . . unless it is beamed from space. Now, if the proper reflecting satellites are launched to redirect beams from earth . . ."

". . . they could hit anything, anywhere, at any time," Carter rasped.

"Exactly."

"That's why Alderstaadt has become ultraimportant," Hawk growled. "Klassen, tell him."

"I managed to get a look at the personnel file on the people who are working in the Alderstaadt bunker. Besides regular telephone technicians, there is a highly specialized team of computer people. They are installing high-speed modems and special equipment to handle ground communications."

"Because we monitor their satellite communications," Carter offered.

"Exactly." Hamm moved to Carter's side and again ran his fingers over the map. "Another theory. It is possible that Gorzow doesn't have the computer capability for such a huge project. Ergo, they transmit their questions to the Gertnoye Research Center outside Moscow and receive instant answers.''

Hawk took the floor. ''If we can tap Alderstaadt, we'll know for sure what's going on there. Best of all, we might be able to piece together the answers they have on the chemical laser and match it.''

''And then?'' Carter asked, already anticipating the answer.

''Knock out or cripple the Gorzow facility until we catch up.''

Klassen gave Carter a three-page, single-spaced report. ''Here is what I've been able to find out about Gorzow and the people in charge, Nick. Study it on your flight back to Berlin, and then burn it.''

''Right.''

''And, Nick,'' Hawk said, ''push your people. Get Alderstaadt on line in two weeks if possible. And get Copperhead before he finds out what we're doing there.''

Carter shooks hands with the professor and Hawk. ''Let's hope that much can be done by tomorrow morning.''

''I'll walk you to the car,'' Klassen said, falling in step behind the Killmaster.

By the time they reached the Mercedes, Carter sensed the anxiety in the other man's manner.

''What is it, Klaus?''

''Trena sends her best.''

''Send mine back. But that's not all of it.''

''No. They picked up our radio operator. That's why I had to come over in person.''

''Oh, my God . . .''

''Don't worry. He killed himself before they were able to interrogate him. But they have put three investigating teams on it. It will take a while, and probably a lot more arrests . . .''

''But it's only a matter of time until the trail leads to the two of you.''

Klaus nodded. ''Let's hope it's long enough.''

"No. Get out now, both you and Trena."

"No, Nick. We'll stay and help you get Gorzow if all this proves to be fact. Then we'll come back out with you."

"Sure," Carter growled. "If I can get back out."

EIGHT

"Poulson?"

"*Ja, mein Herr?*"

"Everything is set?"

"*Ja, mein Herr.* And the exchange with your Colonel Fox?"

"Exactly as we agreed. I shall pick up the copies as usual?"

"Agreed."

Bernard Evers hung up and moved to the apartment's front window. His tail was still across the street, obviously bored but watching the lights Evers had left on in his own apartment below. He only hoped that Colonel Randolph Fox's tail was doing the same.

It had started to rain, a light drizzle, but the forecast was for heavy showers further into the evening.

Evers finished the small brandy and moved into the small alcove that served as a bedroom for the apartment belonging to his alter ego, Dr. Emil Bondorf.

At the narrow closet he pushed aside a wardrobe of suits, dress shirts, and coats, all padded three sizes larger than Evers wore.

A hidden catch in the cedar-paneled wall released spring pressure on a section of the ceiling molding. The two-foot-wide section pulled out like a drawer. From it Evers took a dark turtleneck sweater, a black leather jacket, and matching heavy leather pants. Inside one of a pair of riding boots was a blond wig.

Evers carefully dressed and adjusted the wig over his dark hair. He didn't think it would be necessary, but as an added disguise he spirit-gummed a trimmed, sandy-blond beard and mustache over his own clean-shaven features.

The hall was empty. Evers climbed the final flight of steps and then went up a pull-down ladder to the roof. The rain was coming down harder now as he padded silently across the gravel in stocking feet.

At the edge of the roof he peered over cautiously. Below was a dead-end alley. Across from the alley's open end, he could see the doorway where his watcher slouched out of the rain, cupping the lighted end of a cigarette to hide its glow from being seen through Evers's windows.

"Fool," Evers hissed aloud, and began unhinging the drainpipe where it came to the corner of the building. When this was done, he moved twelve feet back and began swinging the drain out.

Quietly and slowly he swung the pipe, squinting his eyes and concentrating on the narrow break in the brick molding atop the adjacent building. When it was just right, he lowered the edge of the drain and heard it softly settle into position.

When the hinges on his side were securely clicked into place, Evers crawled up onto the pipe on his hands and knees. A one-inch steel rod ran along the bottom of the drainpipe to reinforce it up to 300 pounds. Bernard Evers weighed exactly 160 pounds.

Taking a deep breath, he scurried across the distance and dropped to the other roof.

Again he checked his watcher. There was no need; all

was the same. But even if the man had happened to look up, there was very little chance he could have seen the crawling figure through the rain against the inky-black night sky.

Evers pulled on his boots and trotted across the roof. The four buildings beside his were all connected. Between the last two buildings before the corner was a very narrow alley and a common fire escape.

Removing his boots once again, Evers went down the fire escape and, with a key, let himself into the basement furnace room of the corner building.

In the rear of the boiler that provided heat for that building and its sister structure across the street was a wall trap that opened into a crawlway. The crawlway ran adjacent to the ducts that took the heat across the street to the second building.

It took Evers twenty minutes to negotiate under the street and drop into the basement a full block and one street over from his own apartment building.

An unlocked door led into the second section of the basement, an open, underground garage.

Donning his boots again, Evers quickly strolled to a tarpaulin in the farthest reaches of the garage. Under the tarp was a powerful 500cc BMW. From one of the metal saddlebags he took a six-inch stiletto and slipped it under the skintight leather covering his right forearm. From the other bag he withdrew a darkly visored black motorcycle helmet.

Two minutes later John Byram shrank back into the shadows of his doorway as a big black motorcycle flew by, throwing a spray of water that soaked the bottom of his trousers and his shoes.

"Bastard!" Byram hissed. "I hope you crash somewhere riding like that in this rain!"

He glanced up at the lights that were still on in Evers's apartment, then flipped open his notebook.

7:30 P.M.:Evers in his apartment. No one in, no one out.

And above Byram, in Bernard Evers's living room, an automatic timer on the captain's answering machine clicked in. The machine dialed one of its prerecorded numbers.

Across Berlin, in the Zehlondorf section of the city, Colonel Randolph Fox's wife Ellie picked up the phone.

"Yes?"

Mrs. Fox's voice, and then the millisecond of silence, activated the tape recorder in the machine. "Mrs. Fox, this is Captain Evers. I wonder if I could speak to the colonel?"

"He's not at home at the moment. And I really don't know when to expect him."

"Oh, I see . . ."

"If you'll leave your—"

"Oh, I see. We'll, that's all right. I'll talk to him in the morning."

The phone went dead.

"How rude," Ellie Fox mused, dropping the phone back to its cradle and immediately forgetting the call as the theme song of her favorite television program swelled from a set in the corner of the room.

In the basement of Bernard Evers's building, Monty Pierson, another AXE agent, turned off the tape recorder and picked up a pen to record the call in his log.

7:31 P.M. Evers calls Fox. Fox out. Evers in.

Carter was sure he had no tail, but he took three cabs anyway and sprinted several blocks between each one to get from Tegelhof to the meeting he had arranged with Steve Hardin.

The major was waiting at the bar of a little place on the Lietzenburgerstrasse. He spotted Carter coming in, nodded in reply to Carter's nod, and followed the Killmaster down to the more crowded lower level.

One in front of the other, they wended their way through dancing teen-agers to a table. Seated, they had to lean their heads close together to hear each other's words over the din.

"You got it?"

Hardin slipped a stapled folder from under his coat and set it in front of the Killmaster.

"It's clean, right?"

Hardin lifted his gloved hands. "There's not a print on it."

Carter checked the staples and opened the folder. He couldn't understand a word of what he read, and the charts and graphs were meaningless to him, but it all looked impressive.

"I'd believe it. Would they?"

"For a while," Hardin replied. "It's actual stuff on basic impulse sensors, but if anyone built one from these specs, the damned thing would never work."

"Good enough. Where's the car?"

"Around the corner, a white Volvo two-door. Here are the keys."

Carter pocketed the keys and slid the folder inside his coat. "You've been a big help, Steve. I can't thank you enough."

"Sure I can't do anything else?" Hardin grinned. "I'm beginning to like this."

"You've done enough, and your big job's coming up. See you."

"Wait a minute. Can you give me a hint what all this is about?"

"Sure," Carter said and chuckled. "It's a spook caper. See you!"

He threaded his way back through the milling bodies and up the stairs to the main floor. Once there, he circled around the bar toward a bank of telephones.

Marty Jacobs answered on the first ring.

"How're we doing?"

"Hard to say," came the reply. "Evers is tucked in for the night, it looks like. At last word, Lieutenant Marino was taking a long walk in the rain."

"Any special direction?"

"Not that we can determine. Fox and one of the clerks, a Lieutenant Donovan, are running around. If we get anything, it looks like it will come from one of those three. Everyone else is staying home out of the rain."

"Stay on 'em. I'm about to make the call."

"Will do."

Carter cut the connection and dailed the now well-known number that would bring Poulson on the line.

"*Ja?*"

"Carter here."

"You are three minutes late."

"I had to take a piss. Don't give me a hard time."

"Where are you?"

"A teeny-bopper *Biergarten* on the Lietzen-burgerstrasse."

"Do you have a car?"

"I do . . . a white Volvo two-door."

"Very well. Drive toward Spandau. At the ring, turn north on Schonwalder Allee—"

"That will take me into the Berliner Forest."

"Yes. At Section Forty-two, just before the Oberjager, there is a turnoff to the right. Take it and park. By then it should be nine o'clock sharp. If it isn't, wait in your car until nine."

"Then what?"

"Get out and walk up the path to the fountain. Behind the memorial plate, you will find the instructions for picking up the photos and the master tape—"

"Instructions? Why not just give me the tape and nega-tives then and there?" Carter barked.

"Don't be a fool, Carter. I want an hour for my expert to look over what you have offered to trade. Leave it behind the plate and return to your car. And, Carter . . ."

"Yeah?"

"If anyone follows you into the forest or to the fountain, we won't even bother to pick up your material. I will have a sniper shoot you and we will run."

The line went dead. Carter replaced the receiver and moved through the bar out into the rain.

Fox, Donovan, and Marino are off and running, he thought as he started the Volvo. *Let's hope one of them is running in my direction.*

Elke Zinder always did as she was told. She did this even when the little bit of logic her brain contained told her that the order was wrong or dangerous.

"Just make the delivery," Poulson had said, handing her the negatives and the doctored tape.

"But why me?"

"Because I said so. And besides, don't you want to see the bastard squirm a little after what he did to you?"

She had seen the anger and felt the brutality in this Carter. That was why she had so strongly objected to making the exchange herself and meeting the American alone.

But Franz Poulson had insisted, commanded. And when Poulson commanded, Elke obeyed.

The large, imposing gate was unlocked. The courtyard beyond was dimly lit by an electric lantern hanging from the limb of a tree.

She stepped inside and walked up the narrow gravel path to the darkness of an ornately paneled front door. Light edged around a lace curtain over the door's single panel.

Holding the key Poulson had given her with both hands, she shakily inserted it into the lock.

The door opened on well-oiled hinges and Elke stepped quickly inside. She closed it behind her, leaving it unlocked as she had been told.

Poulson's words echoed in her ears: "Third door on the right, the den. Wait for him in there."

The room was high-ceilinged and book-lined. A huge leather-topped desk and a massive executive chair dominated its center. The whole was lit by concealed strips near the ceiling, evidently on a dimmer turned very low.

She deposited her purse on the desk and started to fumble in the pocket of her coat for cigarettes and lighter.

"Hello, Elke."

She whirled, a scream forming in her throat. It died on her lips and became a sigh when she saw the voice's owner.

"You . . ."

"You look as delicious as ever, *Liebchen*."

"What are you doing here?" she asked, and then emitted a nervous giggle. "And what the hell is the blond hair and the beard and the leather getup for?"

"You, my dear." He had reached her and folded her big body in his arms. "Don't you welcome your old customers better than that?"

"Look, I'm supposed to meet someone here. I don't know what the hell . . . aggggg . . . ."

Her eyes went wide and her mouth slack. A dying shudder went through her body and he let her slip to the floor.

The hilt of the stiletto protruded from just behind her right ear. Around it, a small, thin stream of blood ran down to mat a little of her hair and drip on the carpet.

Carefully he leaned, pulled the blade free, and cleaned it on her dress. Then he used the sharp tip to shred the dress and her underwear. This done, he slipped the stiletto back under the tight sleeve of the leather jacket and trotted toward the rear of the house.

At the wall, he climbed some low, sturdy vines until he could grasp a heavy limb. Like a cat, he swung his lower body up to the limb and crawled to its end. When he was sure it was clear, he dropped silently into the street.

Two blocks away, Bernard Evers kicked the BMW to life and rode into the Berlin night, back to his apartment and a good night's sleep.

The Killmaster turned through the tall stone pillars, crossed the wide parking area, and entered the Berliner Forest. As he moved up the Schonwalder Allee, he narrowed his eyes at the section markers: 18, 30, 36.

When he spotted Number 42 he slowed, dropping the Volvo into second gear.

He spotted the cutoff just as they told him, and turned off. About four car lengths in, his lights hit a chain across the drive. He killed the engine and lights and checked his watch.

It was ten minutes until nine.

A good sweat and two very fast cigarettes later, he slid from the car. As he stepped over the chain and walked up the path, he squeezed his left bicep against the holstered 9mm Luger—a gun he'd long ago named Wilhelmina—under his armpit. Hugo, in his chamois spring sheath, was ready on Carter's right forearm.

If he had to, he would use them, but he was praying it wouldn't be necessary. If it did, the whole week's work would be for naught.

The path widened with a stone bench and a bluish lamp every twenty or so yards.

Carter didn't hurry, he ambled, so it was nearly ten minutes beore he reached the monument. It was a black marble obelisk about thirty feet high, its base encrusted with pigeon guano.

Just above the base, in the obelisk itself, was a bronze plate inscribed in both German and Latin.

The Killmaster ran his fingers around the plate. There was a gap in one side. He could barely feel a sheet of paper in the gap between the bronze and the stone.

A squeeze of his right forearm, and Hugo was in his hand. In seconds, using the blade, he retrieved the paper.

Carter. Put the goods behind the plate. You can pick up yours at the Neiderhof. It's a private residence at 11 Bergenstrasse in Gatow . . . .

"Bastards," Carter hissed under his breath. Gatow was across the Havel River, and one hell of a drive from where he was.

Remember, one hour. Burn this note.

At this point, the pictures, negatives, and tape played no real significant part in his plan. But to keep the game going and the bait strong for Copperhead, Carter knew he would have to go through with the whole thing.

He took the scientific brief from beneath his coat and stuffed it into the gap. He then stood and, holding up the note, touched the flame of his lighter to one corner.

When it had burned to his fingers, he dropped it, waited for the embers to consume the last tiny corner, and stomped on the ashes.

Calmly, lighting a cigarette, he surveyed the dark trees beyond the pool of lights above the monument.

He couldn't resist it.

"Satisfied, bastards?" he called in a loud, clear voice.

Then he trotted back to the Volvo and slid into the driver's seat. He didn't even try the key. Light from one of the bluish lamps flooding through the windshield told him it would be useless.

They were making sure he used up the full hour getting to Gatow.

On the passenger seat was the Volvo's distributor cap, the six ignition wires still attached.

With a groan he pulled the hood latch, grabbed the distributor cap, and climbed from the car.

He was just ducking under the hood when a small, dark sedan rounded the corner of the Oberjager and sped past him with its lights off.

Carter didn't even bother to look up. He didn't have to. It was all too obvious who it was.

NINE

Colonel Randolph Fox got out of his army-issue green sedan and pulled his collar up against the rain. There were puddles of water in the road. Now and then he could hear dogs barking in the distance.

Not a soul was in sight.

He had gotten the tip that afternoon in the Lindenhof, a restaurant where he ate lunch every day. The owner served specialty American dishes for which he often couldn't obtain the required ingredients. In return for supplying those ingredients from U.S. military warehouses, Colonel Fox ate well and often at the Lindenhof. He also received afternoon favors from any waitress who caught his eye.

He was never denied. The girls at the Lindenhof had been warned not to deny the American colonel. If they did, they would be looking for other jobs.

He had been sitting at his regular booth, a private one enclosed with latticework on three sides and a drape across the fourth.

A gourmet lunch had already been devoured, and a fresh cigar and brandy had been delivered by a fresh-faced buxom Fräulein who appeared to be in her late teens. Fox

was just contemplating whether he should return to the
office or take the waitress to a nearby hotel, when a voice
spoke just behind him, beyond the lattice.

"You are Colonel Fox?"

"Yes . . ."

"No, don't turn around, Colonel. If you do, I will not
give you the information you so desire."

The voice was that of an old woman. It cracked and
wavered with age. Her English was heavily accented.

"What information?"

"You are worried about this man, Carter—the colonel
who goes over your head in his command."

Never one to be subtle or cautious, Fox replied at once.
"You're damned right I am."

"We can give you proof that Carter is dealing with the
Federal Republic. We also have the answer to the radar
station that so perplexes you."

Fox's fingers went white around the stem of the brandy
glass. On impulse, he started to turn.

"No . . ."

Fox relaxed. "What do you want in return?"

"A favor, one day soon . . . that is all."

Fox's mind was whirling. Here was a chance to raise
hell with that smart-ass Carter, and find out just what the
hell the boys in the spook department were pulling on him.

With any luck, he could dump the whole thing in the
laps of Congress and become a general in a month.

"Well, Colonel Fox?"

"You have a deal," Fox replied, thinking that, when
the time for the favor came, they could go to hell for it.
"What do I do?"

"This evening at precisely ten, go to Liegerstrasse
Station. Once there, enter the restaurant and take the last
booth on the right near the counter. If the booth is occupied, go into the bar and wait until it is empty. Do you
understand?"

"Of course, dammit. What then?"

"The waiter will have your description. With your coffee he will pass you a key."

"What will the key—"

"Don't rush me, Colonel. The key will fit one of the luggage boxes in Section B of the station."

"And inside the box . . .?"

"Will be the information you require. I am leaving now, Colonel. Do not turn around and do not try to follow me."

Fox heard her move out of the booth. When the shuffle of her shoes receded, he turned. He got a brief glance of a stooped, black-shawled old woman entering the hallway in the rear that led to the rest rooms.

The colonel knew the restaurant's layout. There was no exit through that hallway. The woman would have to come back out the same way she went in.

He bolted in the hallway himself and darted through the door marked *Herren*. There he stopped, peering through a crack in the door. Directly across from where he stood was the door marked *Damen*.

Seconds later a youngish blonde with long legs and dressed in youthful chic emerged. Fox barely noticed her.

"Pardon, *mein Herr*."

It was a round-bellied burgomaster-type with a florid face and rising forehead.

"In a minute," Fox said brusquely, continuing to block the door.

"I beg your pardon, mein Herr. I wish to leave."

Fox pulled his ID from his pocket and waved it in front of the man's face. "American military, CID. Go squat for a few minutes. I'll let you know when you can leave."

The man backed off.

During this exchange, a well-dressed woman of about thirty came out of the women's room.

Fox let her pass without a second look.

Two minutes later a matronly type with a small girl in tow squeezed herself through the door and lumbered up the hall.

Fox waited another fifteen minutes. When no one else emerged, and the burgomaster started yelling in his ear, Fox gave up.

Just as he hit the end of the hall, a Turk in blue coveralls carrying a mop and pail passed him.

Fox paused.

The Turk knocked twice on the door to the *Damen*. When no one answered, he pulled aside a card from a slot on the door to reveal a sign: *Cleaning—please wait five minutes.* Then he opened the door, stoppered it, and went in.

Fox waited a few minutes and followed.

Other than the Turk, the space was empty.

He had been snookered.

The hell with it, he thought. He would go to the station anyway. If there was any chance that it would pay off, it was worth it.

Now Fox leaned into the rain and walked briskly the last block. Just inside the door, he turned left and entered the restaurant.

The booth was empty.

"Bitte, mein Herr?"

The waiter was young, with a scraggly beard and a pockmarked face. His eyes looked vacant, as if the man were drugged. But they seemed to examine Fox carefully.

"Kaffee."

"Bitte."

The coffee came, and Fox waited for a sign. There was none. He picked up the cup and then the saucer.

No key.

He looked around, but he couldn't spot the waiter.

Perhaps, Fox thought, *he needs to check me out*

further, or get the key from someone else before passing it on to me.

He upended the sugar container and put a spoon in the cup to stir.

The key was in the molasses-thick brew.

Fox glanced around him. When he was sure none of the other patrons were giving him a second glance, he tipped the key from the cup into a paper napkin.

Even though Randolph Fox's military career was based in the area of intelligence, the man cared little for the subtleties of the craft, and he rarely practiced what he did know of procedure.

He wadded the napkin in his hand, dropped a bill on the table, and headed for the main room of the station. He spotted the sign for the lockers and moved toward them, openly checking the number on the key.

In seconds, he withdrew a manila envelope from locker 222. His curiosity was immense, but he maintained enough reason to remember that the center of a public train station was not the place to examine the documents he hoped were in the envelope.

Tucking it under his coat, he made tracks for the front exit. As he moved through the glass door, a stocky, square-jawed man in a rumpled suit fell in step behind him.

Fox turned right and practically collided with two young, well-built men.

"Colonel Fox?"

"Yes?"

The man behind him moved in close. Fox could feel his presence right at his elbow.

"We would like to ask you a few questions, Colonel."

Both men flipped open ID holders and held them up for his inspection.

"CIA? What the hell do you want with me? Do you know who I am?"

"We know damned well who you are, Colonel," said the bulky man at Fox's side.

At the same time, he grasped both of Fox's arms in a grip of steel and one of the others retrieved the envelope.

"Our car is right this way, Colonel."

Carter parked the Volvo two blocks from the address and walked the remaining distance. He turned through the gate, started for the front door, and changed his mind.

He was fairly sure that Copperhead and Poulson would go through with their part of the bargain, but years in the business made him hesitant to walk into such a situation naked.

He skirted the house, checking windows. None was open. Near the rear he found a pair of French doors. The room beyond was dark and appeared to be a den or library.

Through the partially opened door of the room he could see dim light in a hallway and a brighter light emanating from a room on the other side of the hall.

The delivery man, Carter assumed, would be waiting for him in that room.

Hugo made short work of the lock, and the Killmaster moved into the pitch-black room and padded to the door. The hall was empty and there wasn't a sound in the house.

He sheathed Hugo and unholstered Wilhelmina from under his left arm as he moved across the hall. Taking a deep breath, he kicked the door clear open and rolled into the room. Up on one knee, the Luger ready in both hands, he swept the muzzle in a full arc.

The room was empty.

Methodically the Killmaster checked the other rooms on the lower level. They, too, were empty.

At the foot of the stairs Carter decided he was wasting his time, but he decided to play it out.

"Is anyone here?"

He waited a few seconds and called out again.

Nothing.

Poulson had obviously decided to take home the whole bacon. The man was going to sell the plans to Copperhead and keep the negatives and tape in hopes of squeezing Carter a little more.

Well, the Killmaster thought with a chuckle, *let him*. The main thing was the pass of the phony plans to Copperhead. If that had been achieved, Poulson, for all Carter cared, could publish the photos in the *Herald-Tribune*.

Planning on leaving the same way he had entered, Carter retraced his steps to the door of the library. He had left the door open.

Now the light in the hall laid a neat path of illumination across the floor. It led right across Elke Zinder's lifeless body on the carpet.

Carter swore under his breath. It was more than a double cross. It was a *double* double cross. Get the plans and get rid of Carter at the same time.

He was about to bolt for the French doors, when the sound of a booted foot scraping in the graveled courtyard outside halted him.

His instincts quickly shifted from being the hunter to the hunted. He ran to the front door. Through the lace-covered front window he saw them: two police vans parked in front of the house, their blue lights throwing lazy circles in the air.

On the balls of his feet, he ran back. As he passed the library he heard a muted grunt and the sound of a man falling.

Carter thought of bulldozing his way through, but he changed his mind when he heard a guttural whisper.

"Hans, are you all right?"

"*Ja*, I fell over something in the dark!"

There were two of them, and the odds were that the "something" was Boom Boom.

As quietly as he could, Carter sprinted to the rear of the

house. There was another hall, the top of the T going to his left and right.

The Killmaster chose left. At the end there was an open window. Without pausing, he dived through, hit the lawn, rolled to his feet, and landed running.

There was no pretense of quiet now as he pounded through the garden, his feet raising hell on the graveled path.

"*Achtung!* There . . . in the trees!"

Carter found himself running parallel to a wall. The rain beat into his face, blurring his vision.

More by instinct than clear sight, he found a tree with a thick limb extending over the wall. He hit the vine on the wall at full tilt and heaved himself up until he could embrace the limb. Then he swung, twice to get enough height, and reached the limb.

Wildly he scrambled to its end. No blue lights in the street. He rolled down from the limb, still holding on with his hands, and then dropped.

"Stay right there. Do not move, and keep your hands in the air. Karl!"

"*Ja?*"

From behind some tall, heavy foliage in front of Carter, a tall, bulky policeman in uniform played a light across Carter's face and stepped forward. The strap of a machine pistol went over his shoulder, and the weapon itself was aimed right at Carter's gut.

"Lean against the wall, mein Herr, and spread your legs . . . wide!"

It came from the man behind him, and Carter did as he was told. While the one called Karl kept him covered with flash and pistol, the other one did a thorough frisk. He even got Hugo.

"He is armed, Karl . . . a blade and a Luger."

"This way, mein Herr, back to the front of the house!"

Carter marched with one behind him and one safely to the side.

Twice now he had underestimated what they would do. And obviously he had helped set himself up. He had wanted to create the image of a maddened, frustrated man when he belted Elke Zinder and trashed her apartment.

He had done that, all right, but he had also given himself all kinds of motive, as well as giving Poulson or Copperhead a way of derailing him.

Four more uniformed officers milled around the front of one of the vans. One of them was holding a manila envelope.

"I think we have caught us a burglar!" Karl crowed.

"Perhaps more than that. There is a woman in the house . . . dead."

"*Mein Gott . . .*"

"What is it?"

"This is her . . . in this photo!"

"Let me see that." The officer with a lieutenant's bar on his collar grabbed the photo and inspected it in the van's headlight. "The flash . . . shine it on his face."

Karl did as he was told, while the inspector held the picture beside the Killmaster's face.

"And you, mein Herr, are the man."

Out of the corner of his eye, Carter could see himself in lustful fornication with what had once been a very vigorous Boom Boom Zinder.

During the night, the clouds had rained themselves out. Now the sky was a clear blue above Berlin as Captain Bernard Evers stepped from his building. He turned right, and with a brisk step marched off, as he did every workday morning, toward his offices.

At the corner kiosk he bought a paper. In front of St. Mark's, he paused as if he were thinking. Finally he made up his mind and entered the cathedral.

In a pew just across from the confessionals, he knelt to pray. There were a few old women in the church, and all of them were near the front, as close to the altar and their salvation as they could get.

No one had entered behind Evers, and there was no one to observe him from the choir loft above.

When he stood, he darted into the booth and drew the curtains. He quickly found the envelope under the cushions and slid it into his belt between his shirt and coat.

A middle-aged woman with a tow-headed youth hanging onto her skirts was passing in the aisle when Evers slipped from the booth.

"The Father won't be hearing confessions until eleven," she announced.

"I know," Evers replied with a benign smile and nod. "I was confessing only to God."

Evers walked away. Over his shoulder he heard the little boy speak.

"An American, Momma."

"I know. Would to God they would all be so religious!"

When in Rome, do as the Romans do. When in Berlin, Bernard Evers did as so many Germans did. He stopped at his favorite bar for a schnapps and his morning coffee.

"Guten Morgen, mein Herr."

"Good morning, Kroger."

Evers set his briefcase on the bar, and while the barman prepared his coffee, the captain strolled back to wash his hands.

He had to wait until an old man finished at one of the urinals and left before he could unlock the towel cabinet and deposit the envelope.

This done, he returned to the bar.

At precisely eight-fifty, Evers finished his schnapps, his coffee, and his paper.

"Guten Tag, mein Herr."

"Until this evening, Kroger."

At nine o'clock, to the second, Bernard Evers sat down at his desk, fully prepared to be stricken with surprise when he learned sometime that morning that his superior, Colonel Randolph Fox, had been arrested for espionage.

TEN

Tegelhof Detention Center was the main holding area for prisoners in West Berlin whose charges were both serious and of a political nature.

Because Carter's papers identified him as a colonel in the U.S. military, and the charge against him was murder, he was taken to Tegelhof. There he was charged and interrogated.

He said nothing, but demanded that his immediate superior officer, General Harley Wells, be informed.

This was about to be done, when a transcription of the tape found with the photos and negatives was handed to the inspector handling the case.

After reading the transcription, the inspector called West German counterintelligence—the BfV—instead of General Wells.

That was why it was three days before the American authorities were informed, and Wells, in turn, informed Marty Jacobs.

"Herr Carter, your counsel is here to see you. Follow me, please."

Carter followed one guard, with a second one close behind him. They moved from the isolated detention area to a wing of interrogation rooms. An elevator took them down to the first floor of the stark, spotless building, and Carter was ushered into a holding room.

There he was stripped naked and his body and clothes were searched. This done, he was handed a plain blue hospital-type gown and taken into a larger room with two doors and one high window.

A four-foot-square table and two chairs were the room's only furniture.

"Sit."

Carter sat, and the guard left, closing the door behind him yet standing behind it so he could observe Carter's every movement.

Two minutes later Marty Jacobs—in a crisp new uniform sporting major's pips and carrying a briefcase—walked into the room.

He sat and remained like a stone until the door was closed and locked.

"Well, ole buddy, you said there might be a little trouble, but I never expected this."

"Can they hear us?" Carter asked.

"No. They watch us"—Jacobs beamed at the man beyond the door with the window—"but they don't eavesdrop."

"Give me a cigarette."

Jacobs pulled cigarettes and a book of matches from his jacket. He held them up in each hand. When the guard nodded, he slid them across the table to Carter.

"When did you become a lawyer . . . and a major?" Carter asked, inhaling deeply.

"At nine o'clock this morning, when Wells called. We'd like to keep this in the family, but it might be hard to keep a lid on it too much longer. What have you told them?"

"Name, rank, and serial number."

"Well, tell one more."

"You tell me first. Anyone take the bait?"

"Fox, whole hog."

Carter nodded. "That figures. Get anything out of him?"

"Not a damned thing, and we've been sweating him in teams since an hour after we picked him up."

"What's your opinion?"

Marty Jacobs leaned back in his chair and sighed. "For real?"

"For real."

"I think we caught a herring. The guy is a louse, a loser, and a whiner. When we showed him the contents of the envelope, he broke down like a baby. Said he wasn't Copperhead and he didn't know shit about anything."

"Where did he make the pickup?"

"A railroad station restaurant. He claims he got the tip from an old lady."

Marty Jacobs expounded on the story that Fox had stuck to since his interrogation had begun.

"As an intelligence officer, Fox would make a good sweeper in the motor pool," Carter groused. "Obviously the old lady became a young one in the can."

"If Fox is telling the truth."

"You think he's not?" Carter asked.

Jacobs shrugged. "Like I say, I think maybe Fox was given a herring. But on the other hand, if Copperhead is as smart as we assume, he could still *be* Fox, and just have a good strong story and act prepared."

"Could be. Hear any ripple from the other side about the sensor plans arriving? That would clear Fox, since he didn't have a chance to make a drop after he picked them up."

"None, but we can't count on that either."

"How so?" Carter asked, lighting another cigarette off the used butt.

"Klaus Klassen tells us that things have changed over there. All of Copperhead's stuff comes over 'Eyes Only.' Just two or three people now get a look-see, and Klaus has no way of peeking.''

"Shit,'' Carter hissed, slamming the table. ''Then we have no way of pinning Fox, beyond making that pick-up.''

"Looks that way. And from the way you got snookered, it's entirely possible that you and he both caught Copperhead's bite.''

"Don't rub it in.''

Jacobs leaned forward. ''Want to fill me in now?''

"Fairly simple,'' Carter said with a shrug. ''I'd guess Copperhead got the word on me, probably from Moscow. But he couldn't take a chance on Poulson's scheme not being fruitful when he heard how I reacted.''

"So he got the papers and set up you with Boom Boom. You're out of the way, and if the sensor plans are real, he's got those too.''

Carter nodded. ''How did the police arrive so providentially?''

"Tip . . . anonymous.''

"Figures.''

"A passerby, didn't want to get involved, but claims he knew the owners were in the south of France and thought it funny that the lights were on.''

"Did you check them out?''

"Yeah. Nothing. Boom Boom had a key to the house on her. Impossible to say how she got it.''

"What about the waiter in the restaurant who passed Fox the key?''

"El disappear-o. Evidently he dumped the key in the coffee, served it, went right out the back door, and kept going.''

"All tied up very neatly,'' Carter growled, mashing out his cigarette. ''How do I get out of here?''

"That's going to be tricky for a couple of days. We've finally got the BfV convinced. They're willing to go along. The local police are a little different. It's murder, and they're not convinced the whole deal isn't for real.''

"You mean Boom Boom tried to blackmail me, and instead of cash I paid her off with a blade in the brain."

"You got it."

"What about forensics on my stiletto?"

"It was clean, but that doesn't mean a thing."

"Jesus," Carter rasped, lighting yet another cigarette. "Pull some diplomatic crap or something and get me out of here. If Fox isn't our man, then Copperhead's still operating, and it's only a matter of time until he comes on to something . . . like maybe the truth about Alderstaadt."

"We're keeping all the others under surveillance, but it's almost hopeless at this point."

"Can we connect Poulson to Boom Boom?"

"Sure, but not on this deal . . . legally, at least."

Carter smiled. "Then do it illegally, as soon as I get out of here."

"You mean squeeze him? Jesus, you're incorrigible. The police will connect you in a heartbeat."

"Right now I'll take my chances. What about Evers?"

"Nothing new. He was home all evening the night it happened. In fact, about the time most of it was going down, he called Fox from his apartment. We've got it on tape."

"Damn. Copperhead's got to be close to us, right on top of us! If he isn't one of the liaison people, then who the hell *is* he?"

"He is," Jacobs replied drily, "one careful, smart son of a bitch."

"Ja?"

"Guten Tag, Emil."

"Ah, Aunt Margaret, it's so good to hear your voice. How is everything? The family?"

"Fine, dear boy, just fine. I got the book, by the way."

"Ja?"

"Terrible. I didn't find a bit of reality in it. Oh, the

writing and the research were fine, exemplary, actually. But the plot was terrible, Emil, not an ounce of truth in it.''

''I am sorry to hear that. I hope the next one I send you is much better.''

''Let us hope so. I shall look forward to receiving it. Good-bye for now, Emil.''

''Good-bye, Aunt Margaret.''

Bernard Evers replaced the phone and leaned back in his chair with a sigh.

So the plans Carter had passed off were phony. He almost expected they would be, but he still had to pass the copies on over on the inside chance they were genuine.

His one chance to find out what was going on inside that radar station was Herman Bachman. And they were keeping all the workers sequestered. Bachman had no way of contacting him through the regular channels, and Evers had no way of getting to Bachman.

He had recommended that they delay putting Alderstaadt on line until he could find out what the Americans were up to and how much they knew, but the stupid bureaucracy had declined.

Evers lit a fresh cigar and paced. He let his mind relax and sift through the problem point by point. Fifteen minutes later he moved back to the phone with purpose.

''Emma?''

''*Ja?*''

''It's me. My compliments, Emma, on finding the Gatow house and obtaining the key.''

''All went well?''

''As near as I can find out. Herr Carter is being detained and I am sure will be arraigned for murder.''

''And Fox?''

''Your acting, as usual, was superb. He took the bait whole. But now I have another problem.''

''*Ja?*''

''I need a body . . . a woman. She should be destitute,

of course, and have no relatives.''

''That should be simple,'' the woman replied. ''One of the state homes.''

''Good. I want you to prepare papers for her under the name of Estelle Bachman. There will be a funeral, of course.''

''When?''

''Sunday.''

''I will get right on it.''

''Thank you, Emma.''

The exchange was abrupt once all the gears started falling in place. It was made in one of the detention center's small, obscure courtyards.

Carter was formally handed over to the BfV from the local police. The investigation of Elke Zinder's murder was declared a counterespionage case, and responsibility for it was given also to the military unit.

Carter stood idly by as the obviously angry warden signed the release papers and stomped away.

The BfV officer waved Carter into the car and sat beside him. Seconds later they were through the large gates and speeding across Berlin.

In the rear, Carter sat smoking silently. He already knew where he was going. That had been decided earlier that morning after the three-way conference between himself, Marty Jacobs, and Lieutenant Colonel Heinrich Karp of the BfV.

''As you Americans say, Herr Carter, I will pull no punches. If what Herr Jacobs has told me is true, I agree you have a major problem. A spy among your own people is extremely serious. But you have operated—not very successfully, I might add—in my domain.''

''That couldn't be avoided, Colonel.''

''Perhaps. But now I want to know everything.''

Carter and Marty Jacobs exchanged a guarded glance. Karp was in the driver's seat and, under the circumstances, he was right; the BfV did deserve to know the truth if they stuck their necks out to get Carter away from the local police and obtain his freedom.

The Killmaster told the man everything, even the real reason for the Alderstaadt radar station.

It worked, and now Carter was on his way to a safe house prepared by Jacobs.

The center city fell away behind them, and then they moved through the forest. They even passed the turnoff where, several nights before, Carter had passed the sensor documents.

It had all been a losing game, and now they had to start all over again.

"Here we are, mein Herr."

It was a small house in the Rust Weg section, isolated and surrounded with trees. Carter had barely stepped from the car when the door was slammed behind him and it drove off.

Jacobs met him at the door. "Welcome home, jail-bird," he said and grinned.

"You're so cheerful," Carter growled. "How much do we have to give Karp?"

"Daily reports. In return he gives us manpower and cooperation."

"And silence?"

"I'm sure of it. He's a good man, Nick. Maybe we should have let him in on it all from the beginning."

"Hindsight sucks. Wilson and Hardin here?"

"In the living room. So's the scotch. C'mon!"

It was more cottage than full-scale house, but more than big enough for their needs.

Carter shook hands all around and gratefully accepted a drink Steve Hardin had already built for him.

"Welcome to the spook fraternity, gentlemen," Carter drawled, and downed half the drink in one swallow. "How's Crown Prince?"

"We're eighteen feet down and sixty-five over," Jim Wilson replied.

"That means you're almost to the wall."

"Right."

"Did you bring everything?"

"Everything . . . workers, supplies, equipment, every detail."

"Then let's get to work," Carter sighed. "In this mess somewhere there's a needle Copperhead has buried. We've got to find it."

"What about Poulson?" Jacobs asked.

"Tonight," Carter said. "We'll see Herr Poulson tonight."

ELEVEN

Fräulein Emma Dunmetz was a tall woman in her early thirties, with thick, glossy raven hair tied in a prim, tight knot at the nape of her slender neck.

Emma usually wore extremely expensive and fashionable clothes that accentuated her trim figure. Even now, in the crisp, form-fitting nurse's uniform, it was difficult to hide the fluid movements of her trained dancer's body.

She didn't try. The young orderly at the desk would be much less likely to question her papers if his mind were on her high, jutting breasts and her sensuous hips.

"*Guten Tag.*" She smiled warmly. "I am from the Hautfenner Institute. I believe they called you."

"Ah, yes, Fräulein. Here is the file. Clara Feiffer, no known relatives, destitute. Cause of death, liver deterioration. You have the papers?"

"Of course."

The young orderly accepted the papers and returned Emma's beautiful smile.

"You are . . . Nurse . . . ?"

"Helga Klinger, right there," Emma said, nodding toward the papers. "I am authorized to sign the release."

"Ah, yes, I see, I see," the young man jabbered as he glanced through the papers, every now and then stealing a sidelong look at the nurse's astounding figure. "You have transportation?"

"Right outside, one of the Institute's ambulances."

"Good. Well, then, if you'll just sign right there, Fräulein, we can complete this unfortunate business."

"Of course."

"You were certainly fast on this one," he commented as she scrawled her signature over the proffered forms. "Usually the Institute doesn't pick them up for five or six days. We just got this one in this morning at nine."

Emma shrugged.

She herself had picked up the police report on finding the derelict woman's body at six that morning. The false papers from the Hautfenner Institute had been prepared two days earlier, along with the identity papers of Estelle Bachman.

"There you are."

"Danke, Fräulein. Right this way."

Emma followed him into the depths of the building and eventually into the morgue itself.

"It's good work they do at the Institute," he rambled as they walked. "Rather gruesome way for all these to end up, but I imagine that if they knew about it they wouldn't mind . . . helping science and all, you know."

"Yes. Which box is hers?"

"This one." The young man pulled open the drawer and, in almost the same motion, pulled the sheet from the woman's naked, wrinkled body.

"Beat-up old thing, wasn't she?" he commented.

"Yes, quite," Emma responded coolly. "But we're more interested in the inside than the outside."

"Ja, ja. That is true, of course." He flicked another sidelong glance at Emma. The orderly usually got a rise out of the Institute nurses he did this to. One had even fainted.

Not this one.

This one's eyes looked down at the body totally devoid of any emotion. Her face didn't alter expression, and her eyes were like two dots of cold blue ice.

"If you'll fetch a gurney, we'll get her up to the ambulance immediately."

"*Ja, ja, Fräulein*. Right away," the young man replied, feeling a shiver run up his own spine as he looked into those cold blue eyes.

By the time the gurney was unloaded and the young orderly had returned to his desk, he had calmed down.

He was glad he hadn't tried to get the cold-eyed nurse into bed.

It would have been like sleeping with one of his customers.

Dusk was falling outside when they finally took a break and sat down to the meal prepared by the resident housekeeper.

"I think we're safe," Wilson said, cutting into his veal with relish.

"Don't feel too secure," Carter replied. "This guy is established. He's got people everywhere."

"But, Jesus, Nick, we've checked *everything*, right down to the shredder that does away with the equipment orders! Everything fits, and there can't be a leak."

"There can always be a leak. Trena Klassen told me that everything Copperhead passes is gold. He's privy to everything the BfV *and* our intelligence people do. If he's that high up, he can put somebody close to Crown Prince."

"Then what do we do next?" Marty Jacobs asked with a yawn.

"The three of you go all over it again while I have a little talk with our friendly pimp, Poulson."

Emma Dunmetz stepped from the front of the ambulance dressed in a black cashmere skirt and jacket, a conservative white blouse, gloves, and carrying a briefcase.

The bell had barely tinkled above the door when a short, fat man with sad eyes and thinning hair appeared as if by magic from the bowels of the funeral parlor.

"May I help you, Fräulein?"

"I am Frau Ernestine Leffler, counselor for the Bachman estate."

"Ah, yes, Frau Leffler. My assistant told me that you had called from Mainz. Er, the deceased . . . ?"

"At your unloading dock in the hospital ambulance," Emma replied, setting her briefcase on a nearby table and opening it. "I have the death certificate here, as well as the release from the hospital in Mainz."

"Good, good. Will you want the chapel services here?"

"There will be no formal rites, only a short graveside service."

"As you wish," the man replied, his face sinking. Rental of the mortuary chapel was all profit, and a great deal of it.

"Burial will be in the Friedhop Spandau-Sud. Here is the plot number."

He glanced at the paper, then looked up, his brow furrowed. "Sunday? But it is now late Friday evening . . . my embalmer, my assistants are gone . . ."

"Did not your assistant tell you that you would be paid double for this inconvenience?"

"Er, no, he did not. Indeed, he did not." The little mortician had to freeze his face to keep it from smiling.

"You will. There is one more thing. Frau Bachman has a nephew. He is her only living relative. Here is where he can be reached. I have to return to Mainz this evening. I would appreciate it if you would inform Herr Herman Bachman by special messenger of his aunt's demise and interment."

"Of course, of course," he nodded, folding the slip of paper and adding it to the others she had given him. "Will there by anything else, Frau Leffler?"

"That will be all I require of you," Emma stated, handing across another envelope and then snapping the briefcase closed. "Here is a bank draft for your usual fee. Please bill my offices in Mainz for the remainder."

"Certainly, certainly, I shall do just that." The little man smiled, bowing effusively as he showed her to the front door. "Good evening, Frau Leffler. It has been a pleasure."

"Guten Abend, mein Herr."

Franz Poulson lived on Reiswerder, an island in the middle of the channel where the Tegeler See flowed into the Havel River. Marty Jacobs's description of Poulson's estate was all Carter had to go on, but he guessed it would be enough.

The house was a three-story, twenty-room affair sitting on about six acres. It had a high barbed-wire fence around all three of the inland sides. The fourth side was open, fronting on the lake, and was patrolled by armed guards.

Before leaving the safe house, the Killmaster had dressed in a black wet suit and armed himself with a throwaway silenced Mauser that couldn't be traced. In his oilskin boot he also carried a Curai commando knife.

Jacobs had also supplied him with an old Mercedes, which Carter now turned off the main road toward a marina. Just above a long pier jutting out into the lake, he halted the car and climbed out.

It was a starless night, with frothy clouds skudding like lazy gulls over a half moon. To his right and far out into the lake, he could just make out the island. Just in front of him was a graduated stone walkway down to the pier. Other than the muted sound of radios on the bobbing boats, all was quiet.

He moved to the rear of the Mercedes, then unlocked

and lifted the trunk lid. From the trunk he took a small box of sound effects explosives and a rubber raft. With these tucked under his arms, he moved out along the pier.

Everything was as Jacobs had described. At the very end, a tiny light burned in an old green boathouse. Just outside the door, lazily easing himself back and forth in a rocker, was a gray-haired old man sucking on a pipe.

Beyond the old man, gently rocking against its mooring lines, was a twenty-foot yawl. Carter couldn't see the nameplate on the bow of the yawl, but he knew it would read *Kobold*—German for goblin.

He stopped directly in front of the old man, who glanced up with only his eyes. The man's gaze took in the small box and the deflated raft in Carter's arms, and then he spotted the holstered Mauser under the Killmaster's left armpit.

"I am the man," Carter said in German.

Another nod, and the old man carelessly rapped his pipe against the leg of the rocker.

"We go now?"

"Now," Carter replied, and walked toward the yawl.

Seconds later he heard the man drop to the deck behind him. As if they had worked together for years, Carter went to the bow, unasked, and cast off the line. The old man dropped both stern lines, and together they rolled sail. The breeze was not stiff, just healthy enough to fill the sails. At the wheel, the old man put the yawl with the wind and they glided silently into the lake.

"You know the place?" Carter asked.

"*Ja*," the old man growled, sucking on his dead pipe. "On the south end there is an outcropping of rocks, big ones. I can land you about two hundred yards into the lake, just off those rocks. There, you can get ashore without being seen."

"And you?"

"I will give you twenty minutes, and then I will run

aground at the north end of the property.''

"Good man," Carter said, and moved to the raft.

It was double-cored, with four compressed-air canisters, two in each layer. Carter triggered the canisters one by one, and within minutes the raft was inflated. Attached inside were two aluminum oars; one sharp yank and a twist opened them to six-foot oars. These he placed in the rubber oarlocks, secured them, and dragged the raft to the stern of the boat. When the small box of sound effects explosives was also attached to the raft, he returned to the old man.

"Are you sure they won't do anything to you?"

"Nothing," he replied. "Where I am going in, there is a jetty of rocks maybe one or two feet above the surface. Normally, there is a buoy light. My son extinguished it earlier this evening. They can say nothing. It will be an accident."

"You will be highly paid."

The old man's weather-beaten face cracked a smile. "I already have."

Carter returned the grin, slapped the old man on the back, and walked to the stern. He sat on the edge of the raft, lit a cigarette, and cupped it as he smoked. They were still nearly a mile from the island, but he could see it growing larger with each passing minute.

It was a mystery as to what he could get out of Poulson. The man was a free-lancer, obviously. He did deal with the BfV, and also American intelligence, supplying both with bits and pieces. But now it was an established fact that he also dealt with the East and Copperhead.

There was a slight chance—probably none at all—that the saloon keeper/pimp knew the East German agent's real identity. But Carter had already counted on that. What he hoped to gain this night was the means Poulson used to contact Copperhead and vice versa.

The swift-moving little boat rolled to port, and Carter

looked up at the wheel. The old man held up his hand, the fingers spread wide. He squeezed it into a fist and released it again.

Ten minutes, Carter thought, and extinguished his cigarette. He lowered the stern rail, then slid the raft out over the water about three feet. This done, he crouched behind it and rolled his eyes around to watch the old man's silhouette against the dim sky.

It seemed an eternity, but at last he saw an arm raised and a solitary finger make a circular motion.

He pushed off, and just as the tip of the raft hit the water, he launched himself into the air. When the bottom of the raft made a soft thud in the water, Carter belly flopped into its center.

He let the pull of the yawl drift him for a couple of minutes, but then he anchored his feet in the rubber hooks and began to row. The little boat had been specially made for just this type of landing. Carter was able to keep up a brisk speed while hardly lifting his shoulders or head above the sides of the raft.

From the shore he would appear to be a floating piece of debris.

Now and then he would pause, bend his eyes toward the island, and then glance at the illuminated dial of his watch. For the next fifteen minutes he rowed and paused, rowed and paused, rowed and paused.

Then he saw the rocks.

When he was within thirty yards he anchored the oars and rolled into the water. A loop had already been made in the short bowline. He moved this over his head and shoulders until it was secure around his chest, and began a strong, steady breast stroke. In no time he was at the rocks. More by feel than sight did he find a break in them wide enough to haul himself, and then the raft, ashore.

Carefully, keeping himself and the raft out of sight, he moved through the rocks. Eventually he found a place wide enough to store the raft. When the small box of explosives was securely attached to the black web belt around his waist, he moved through the remainder of the rocks right to the edge of the beach and checked his watch again.

Twenty minutes minus ten seconds.

He waited the ten seconds and two minutes more, and then dropped into the sand. His feet had barely hit, when from some distance away he heard angry shouts and saw the glow of flashlights throwing their beams out into the lake.

The old man was right on the nose.

Crouching, Carter moved up the beach and into the trees where he dropped to one knee and listened.

The angry shouts from the lake had now diminished to a more conversational level. Carter could barely make out men in the water trying to push the *Kobold* off the rocks.

The house loomed above the trees about a hundred yards on. Between it and Carter was a small pool house surrounded by manicured gardens.

He moved forward, then stopped abruptly when he saw the glow of a cigarette out of the corner of his right eye.

The guy was big, about Carter's size. He was leaning against a tree and looking out toward the lake. A machine pistol hung over his shoulder, and a Mauser like the one Carter held in his own hand was stuck in the waistband of his trousers.

Herr Poulson, Carter thought, *has one hell of a lot of enemies.*

The Killmaster was about to circle around the man, when he heard boots crunch gravel nearby and a second man joined the first.

"Peter?"

"*Ja.*"

"What is it?"

"An old man grounded his boat on the rocks. The buoy light was off."

"Jesus, did you fix it?"

"*Ja*, and we got the old fool off the rocks. I'm not even going to tell Poulson. He'll just chew us out for forgetting to check the light at dusk."

"*Ja. Kaffee?*"

"*Ja, danke.*"

The two men moved off toward the pool house, and Carter sighed with relief. He waited until they were inside, and then he followed the tree line until he was near the house.

Lights blazed in every first-floor window and from several rooms on the second and third floors. He could see through the kitchen window. A man sat at a table, reading a paper and sipping coffee. An older woman in a domestic's uniform worked at a counter.

Carter moved on. There were two other men in the house, walking around slowly. It was just Poulson's breed to surround himself with an army, Carter mused.

The front of the house, other than the first floor, was dark. Near the corner Carter spotted what he wanted: a tree that reached nearly to the roof with several branches that scraped the side of the building.

The Killmaster took the box from his belt and opened it. Then he retraced his steps down the side of the building. At each window he mashed one of the little suction cups attached to the charges. He set the timers for thirty minutes and returned to the tree.

Just before climbing the tree, he removed a thin slice of plastique from the box and fastened it inside the boot not containing the knife.

Then he started to climb.

Friday nights Franz Poulson reserved for his personal pleasure. He had long made it a rule not to involve himself with any of the women who worked for him. But he was a man like other men; he needed women. But not just any other women.

Poulson craved the women that all men wanted but could not attain.

Fatima was such a woman. She had been brought in from Casablanca by Poulson's rival club owner in Berlin, Albert Butz. For the last month, Butz had tried to seduce the star of his Middle Eastern floor show.

Butz had been thwarted. Franz Poulson wouldn't be. Secretly he had wined and dined this Moroccan beauty, and now he had wooed her to his house for a private performance.

After the performance? Well, who knew?

But few women turned down Franz Poulson.

Before him, the woman arched her body in a sensuous pose. Her eyes flashed both defiance and desire. Under the shimmering skirt and bra, her body moved snakelike to the sounds of the desert coming from the room's stereo speakers.

"You know, Franz, I have never danced privately before, not even for a sheik."

"I know. That is why I pursued you so hard to dance for me," Poulson replied with a dry smile, his eyes flickering over every curve and hollow of her sensuous body.

"You are positive that you can get me papers to stay in Berlin?—To live here?"

Poulson sighed, and then smiled. It was the one thing Fatima wanted above money: German citizenship. With it she could make more money in one year than she could make in a lifetime in Morocco.

Butz couldn't get it for her. Franz Poulson could.

"The papers will be yours by tomorrow this time. Now dance for me, entice me . . . seduce me!"

Suddenly she shouted, jumped straight into the air, and descended with her feet wide apart. At the end of her long brown arms her fingers twisted like tentacles, and the sound of tiny brass cymbals joined the exotic music in the room.

Undulating like a serpent, she whipped her body around and around the seated man. Gauze veils trailed her spinning torso, and lusty fire seemed to shoot from her dark, heavily kohl-lined eyes. Her bare feet seemed to hardly touch the ground, and now and then in passing she would lean forward to flail his face with her dark hair.

Suddenly she stopped directly in front of him, her legs spread wide, hands on hips. Her body was motionless except for the rhythmic rise and fall of her belly muscles. They rolled and undulated as she seemed to control them individually. The lower abdomen remained still, then small ripples of flesh would begin high under the ribs, rolling precisely downward with consummate ease.

Slowly, Poulson's hands came up. He touched the clasp beneath the dark valley of her breasts, and suddenly they burst free. With a smile she shrugged the bra from her shoulders and whirled away from him again. For a good five minutes she mesmerized him with the dance. As the sheen of perspiration came over her whole body, she moved back to him, this time turning to her side. Again she became motionless. Then, slowly, her hips began to move to and fro, toward him, and away.

Poulson was breathing heavily now. He looked up and saw the meaning in her eyes. Again his hands came forward. They found the clasp of her skirt, and just as it fell free she whirled in a perfect circle, again coming around to face him. She arched her back and leaned her pelvis forward, at the same time squeezing her voluptuous breasts together with her arms.

Poulson came to his feet. "Now?" he growled.

"Now," she whispered, and opened her arms to him.

It took Carter fifteen minutes to locate the third-floor sitting room. He did it first by trial and error, and then by following the eerie music and jingling finger cymbals.

Just as Jacobs had predicted, Poulson was entertaining.

Struggling with both the steely-eyed blond man and the woman would make the whole thing just that much more convincing.

The girl was just moving her naked body into Poulson's arms when the Killmaster stepped through the door and closed it gently behind him.

The sound of a shell being jacked into the Mauser's firing chamber alerted Poulson. He flung the girl from him, and without even registering the intruder, he lunged toward a shoulder rig he had discarded earlier and had hung over the back of a nearby chair.

Two long strides brought Carter in line, where he hip-blocked the other man. Poulson grunted from the sudden pain in his ribs and rolled away. When he came up on one knee for another try, Carter raised the Mauser.

"Don't. It's silenced. Your goons down below won't hear a thing. You'll be dead and I'll be gone before they ever know."

The girl had come to her feet and stood frozen during the melee. Now Carter saw her begin to thaw out. Her full breasts expanded, her throat tightened, and her mouth opened wide to scream.

Carter barely got his forearm over her face in time. As it was, she managed to get out a pretty loud squawk. The Killmaster started to move his forearm to her throat, when Poulson made his move.

He came up off the floor like a cat, grabbing Carter's wrist. The Killmaster squeezed off one shot and the slug slammed harmlessly into the wall. Poulson tried to bring Carter's arm down over his knee, but he found Fatima all over him like a blanket before he could do any damage.

Her weight on his arms, shoved down harder by Carter, broke the man's hold. Both of them tumbled to the floor, and Carter was on them in an instant. He grabbed her by the hair and jerked her head back. At the same time, he ground the snout of the Mauser's silencer into Poulson's throat.

"Lie still and don't make a sound!" he breathed into the woman's ear.

"Franz . . ." the girl gurgled.

"Be quiet and do what he says."

"Better, much better."

"What do you want?"

"Copperhead. Who is he?"

"I don't know what you're talking about."

"Bullshit. The stuff I passed you got into a Colonel Fox's hands. Is he Copperhead?"

"I still don't know—"

"Franz, he's hurting me!"

"Shut up!" Poulson gagged as Carter ground the silencer harder into his windpipe.

"Talk to me, Poulson! I'm not just an army colonel. I'm one bad son of a bitch and I'll shoot you in a second. Or didn't Copperhead tell you who I was?"

There was fear on the blond man's handsome face now, and sweat had popped out in beads on his forehead.

"I swear it! I don't know who he is. I just did what I was told to do!"

"You're scum, Poulson, real scum." Carter twisted the girl's body off Poulson's, and stood.

"Get up!"

Poulson came to his feet. He acted whipped, but Carter knew he wasn't. The man was a waiting adder, just poised to strike.

A quick glance down told Carter he had one minute left until the charges went off at the windows. When they did, there would be mass chaos on the floors below and in the garden.

"You've got ten seconds, Poulson. Who is Copperhead?"

"Damn you, I swear I don't know!"

Carter moved toward him. "Then you're dead."

"You crazy bastard. I sell him information. I sell the

Americans informations, the Russians, everybody! But all I have is contacts. I never see anybody, I swear . . .''

Bingo, Carter thought, and shoved the man up against the wall by the neck.

He sensed the girl moving behind him but paid very little attention. If she didn't make a move, he would have to find some way for Poulson to make it without seeming obvious.

He didn't have to. He saw the shadow of the lamp coming up on the wall. And then the blow came, too low at the base of his neck to do much damage, but he faked it well. The gun slipped from his hand to clatter to the floor, and he stumbled forward against Poulson.

His estimation of the man was correct. Poulson's reflexes were indeed those of a venomous snake. His right fist caught Carter square in the gut, and was quickly followed by a left. As the Killmaster went over, the other man's knee came up into his face. Carter managed to turn his head and take most of the blow on the side of his face and shoulder. At the same time, he fell away and collapsed on the floor.

Then all hell broke loose. The sound of explosions and shattering glass, quickly followed by shouting voices, filled the house.

"Gott in Himmel!" Poulson cried.

He stopped for just a second to make sure Carter was out, then bolted for the door, grabbing both the Killmaster's and his own gun along the way.

"What is all this?" the girl screamed. "Don't leave me with him!"

Poulson paid no attention and shot through the door.

Carter cautiously slitted one eye. The naked girl bounced from one foot to the other, her fearful eyes looking from him to the door and back again. He held his breath, waiting.

She didn't move.

He groaned and started to rise. The sound and the movement was like added fuel to a flaming rocket. She grabbed her skirt and bra with a shriek, and followed Poulson through the door.

Carter rolled to his butt, twisted the heel of his right boot, and let the tiny bug drop into his hand. He used the Curai knife like a screwdriver on the two screws of the telephone. The plate came only partially off, but it was far enough to plant the magnetic bug.

Seconds later—with the thud of boots coming up the stairs—the screws were in place, the knife was in his boot, and Carter was back on the floor.

It was a gamble, but a safe one. If Carter was right, Poulson would try to sell him to Copperhead. To do that, he had to make a contact. Marty Jacobs had the estate covered from the front in case a messenger was sent.

By planting the bug, Carter had covered the other means of communication.

TWELVE

Herman Bachman was not an intellectual giant, but he could reason and he knew his trade.

Each morning since the job had begun, they would load him and his fellow workers in vans and herd them to the site. Usually they would go right into the tunnel. But this morning they had been delayed topside because of a foul-up the previous evening: the crates of equipment hadn't arrived the night before. Consequently, the dirt from the previous day's digging had not been removed in the empties.

With the others, Bachman had stood around smoking and sipping coffee while Major Wilson supervised his people. It was the first time Bachman had been privy to the actual process of the dirt removal.

It was also the first time he had gotten a glimpse of what type of equipment came out of the boxes before the dirt was put in.

Mentally he noted each piece. There were miles of cable, telecommunication reception equipment, wire and tape recorders, drills, torches, and blasting gear.

Bachman couldn't know exactly what the ultimate purpose of the tunnel or the equipment would be. But he could see the direction in which they were digging and where the cables were going to go once the tunnel was finished: under the wall.

Now, this Saturday evening, he had it all, everything he assumed Copperhead needed about the so-called radar station. It would be up to the master spy himself, whoever he was, and the people who supervised him to put all the pieces of the puzzle together. Herman Bachman didn't reason; he just observed and reported.

The problem that faced Bachman this Saturday dusk as he remained aloof from his coworkers in the rocking van, was how to report what he now knew as facts.

There was no way to get word in or out of the area where he lived and was watched night and the little part of the day when he wasn't working at the site. Of course he could wait until the job was completed and then get his intelligence to Copperhead in his own time. But the man had been insistent: now, as soon as possible, he had to know what the radar station's real use was going to be.

Inside the tall wire fence of the compound, Bachman left the van and walked to the mobile home unit that had been assigned to him.

"Bachman?"

"*Ja?*"

It was the boss major, Hardin. The man was striding toward him from the trailer he used as an office.

"I'm afraid I've got some bad news."

"What is it?"

"It's your mother."

"My mother? What about her?"

"She died a couple of days ago. The funeral will be tomorrow at the cemetery in Spandau-Sud."

It took only a couple of blinks for Bachman to react properly, even though this astounding revelation had taken him quite by surprise. He turned from the major's stare and dropped to the steps of the trailer and covered his face with his hands.

"My mother . . . my mother . . ."

"Sorry," Hardin said, laying his hand consolingly on Bachman's shaking shoulder. "We'll let you go, of course."

"*Danke*. It is very kind of you."

"But you will have to be escorted, for security reasons."

Bachman nodded without raising his head or uncovering his eyes. "Of course. I understand."

"Like I say, I'm sorry. I'll have a two-man escort pick you up around eight in the morning. The funeral is at ten. They'll make sure you get there in plenty of time."

"*Ja, ja,* thank you . . . *danke.*"

Hardin walked away and Bachman entered his trailer. Only when the door was securely closed behind him did he smile.

His mother was an old whore in Hamburg. He had not seen the woman in more years than he could remember. If the bitch was dead, going to her funeral was the last thing he would do.

Copperhead was a genius.

Bachman got a beer from the tiny refrigerator and pulled the leather engraving equipment from his bag. He sipped the beer and carefully laid the engraving tools out on the table.

It would be a long night, composing his report and then writing it out on the jacket of the Bible.

It would be a long night, but a very profitable one.

First he would use the invisible shading ink to highlight the words of his report in the verses. Then he would engrave the proper keys on the leather cover of the Bible.

Yes, it would be a long night. But come morning, Herman Bachman would be twenty thousand deutsche marks richer.

Emma Dunmetz was just turning off the lights in the small dance studio she ran as a front and cover, when the private-line phone rang in the upstairs apartment. Taking her time, she walked up the narrow stairs and moved into the small quarters.

"*Ja?*"

"This is Poulson."

"I told you not to call this number—*ever*—unless it was an emergency," she replied, tapping a blood-red nail on top of the glass table.

"This is an emergency, Fräulein. I must get in touch with him at once."

"We have an operation in progress. It is impossible right now."

"This is important, I tell you!" Poulson cried, revealing the amassed tension he felt in his voice. "They might have made me!"

"Who has made you, Franz? For God's sake, you're taking money from every side!"

"But not lately. Lately, only from you."

"No matter. Who is it?"

"The agent, Carter."

"What about him?"

"He must have somehow gotten off the murder charge. He's loose. He came here."

The nail stopped tapping. "When?"

"Last night. I have been trying to contact you. He threatened to kill me unless I told him the identity of Copperhead."

The woman chuckled. "That's hardly possible. None of us knows who Copperhead is."

"He wouldn't believe me."

"Then why are you still alive, Franz?"

"You bitch, I'm alive because I managed to overcome him. He is my prisoner here at the house."

"On the island?"

"*Ja.* I want to know what is to be done with him. It was you and Copperhead who wanted him out of the way in the first place. I only wanted to blackmail him. Now, God knows what he has told his people and what they plan for me. I am afraid to keep him here too long in case they come for him.''

''Offhand I would say kill him, but I will pass your information along and he will call you.''

''When?''

''Not until Monday.''

''Damn!'' Poulson roared. ''Monday could be too late! They could come for him by then!''

''Then kill him now, and dispose of the body. If his fellow agents come for him, deny everything.''

''Damn you . . . and him! I didn't count on this—''

''Good night, Herr Poulson.''

''Wait . . . don't hang up, you bitch—''

Emma dropped the receiver back to its resting place, lit a cigarette, and moved into her dressing room. Carefully, she took the old woman's clothes from her closet and arranged them on the bed.

It was as the old woman that Emma would make the pickup tomorrow from Herman Bachman.

A little more than a mile from the gates of Franz Poulson's island estate, a dark gray, lightless van sat on the shoulder of the road. A red rag was attached to the antenna, telling any inquisitive passerby or police that the van had experienced a breakdown and the driver had left to seek help.

In the soundproof rear of the van, Marty Jacobs nervously sucked on a cigarette as he intently watched the wall of equipment and the two men operating it.

Carter's microrelay bug had been activated three times. The first two times proved to be strike-outs. One of them had been Poulson's lieutenant calling his mistress. The second had been the cook using the kitchen extension to call her son.

The third time was gold.

Anxiously, Jacobs watched one of the operators stop

and start the tapes, going back and forth over the clicks as the phone had been dialed.

"How's it coming?"

"Close . . . one more number . . . shhh!"

Again the tape was rewound and Jacobs sighed with relief when the pencil in the man's hand began to scribble.

"I've got it . . . seven-eight-one-four-four-five."

Jacobs was already reaching for a mobile phone. The line was open and ready.

"Harry?"

"Right here," replied the man Jacobs had placed inside the West German telephone terminus complex.

"We've got it . . . seven-eight-one-four-four-five."

"It will take a few minutes."

"Hurry it up as fast as you can."

"Will do."

Jacobs covered the mouthpiece and spoke to one of the operators. "Get up in the cab and get ready to get us out of here!"

The man moved forward and settled into the driver's seat. Jacobs lit a fresh cigarette from the dying butt of the old one, and sweated.

The woman had told Poulson to kill Carter. Marty Jacobs hoped they got the owner of the telephone number's name and address before the man decided to take action.

"Marty?"

"Yeah, right here."

"It's an unlisted number paid through a post office box. It's registered to Emma Dunmetz at Forty-four Bergenstrasse in Rudow. There's also a business number at the same address, a dance studio."

"Thanks, Harry, see you." Jacobs slammed the phone down and reached for the radio microphone. "Unit Three, did you monitor?"

"Roger, Marty. We're about fifteen minutes from

Rudow and on our way.''

"Good. Do you have a burglar-bugging team with you?''

"We do.''

"Keep them on standby, even if the woman doesn't go out until morning. And make sure there's no one else in there before they go in. If she isn't Copperhead, we want her to lead us to the snake.''

"Righto.''

"Main, come in!''

"Here, Marty.''

"Get me everything anybody's got on Emma Dunmetz, and fast!''

"You got it.''

"Unit Two!''

"We're in place, Marty, about two hundred yards the other side of the gate from you.''

"Is the gate mined?''

"To blow on command.''

"Okay, I'm activating Carter's pulse unit . . . now.''

Jacobs flicked a switch on the console, and a tiny red light started blinking.

"Okay, let's go get him!''

They had placed him in a windowless attic room, with only one locked door. The furniture was sparse: a heavy old bed, a dresser, and one chair.

How long had it been? Twenty-four hours?

At least.

Twice, they had come into the room: the first time with a tray of cold food; the second to lead him down the hall to a bathroom.

Perhaps the gamble had been too big. Maybe Poulson *didn't* know how to contact Copperhead. Maybe there was a prearranged contact time, and Copperhead himself did all the contacting.

Carter stretched out on the bed and wished for a cigarette. They had taken his lighter along with the weapons.

Suddenly he felt it.

Carter came instantly to his feet when the pulser in the hollow heel of his right shoe began to throb against his heel. He pushed the heel to the side and flipped a tiny switch.

Immediately the throbbing stopped and the Killmaster knew that the red light in front of Marty Jacobs now glowed steadily. It would tell Jacobs that he, Carter, had gotten the go-ahead.

He took the thin strip of plastique from his left heel and carefully worked it around the door and into the crack by the lock. Once this was done, he produced a tiny detonator from the hollow heel and then closed it for the last time.

The detonator was no bigger than a safety pin, and shaped like one. Before setting it, he rolled the bed onto its side and planted all of the furniture against it.

This done, he went back to the door. He unhinged the pin, shoved it into the plastique, and hurried to the safety of his nest behind the bed and mattress.

It was a fifteen-second timer, activated eventually by the melting of the outer plastic core over the fuse to release the chemical.

Slowly, Carter counted. At thirteen, he put his head between his knees and his hands over his ears.

The explosion was deafening. It jammed the dresser against the mattress and the mattress over Carter.

It took him only a few seconds to squirrel himself around and get his feet against the bed. With his back to the wall, he pushed until he could see light above one corner of the bed, then pushed harder until the opening was large enough to squeeze through.

The light he saw was moonlight.

Besides the door and a good section of the wall, the plastique had taken out a corner of the roof.

The furniture was kindling. Carter picked up one of the chair legs and darted into the hall. He could hear footsteps pounding up the stairs. He paused.

Only one man.

The stairs turned sharply into the hallway. Other than the moonlight flooding through the roof and what was left of the wall, there was no illumination.

Carter turned his back to the stairs and flattened his side to the wall, with the chair leg an extension of his arms.

When he heard the man's panting wheeze just behind his right shoulder, he swung with all he had in a one-eighty arc.

The chair leg splintered, but so did the face.

The Killmaster caught him before he fell down the stairs, then he threw him to the floor of the hall.

A quick frisk produced a Walther P-1 with a full magazine and one in the chamber. Carter clicked off the safety and headed down the stairs.

Just as he hit the bottom step he heard an ear-shattering explosion in front of the house. Jacobs's boys had done their job. The gate was blown.

Carter bolted down the hall. He was on the third floor. Somehow he had to get down two flights of stairs and toward the front of the house, and he had to do it fast.

He made the second floor and was halfway around the stairwell to the next flight, when a door opened three feet in front of him and a man stepped out.

There was no time to stop. They collided, and both went down, Carter in the center of the hall, the man behind a small table. The Walther slipped from Carter's hand and skidded across the floor. Before he could dive for it, the other man had come to one knee and pulled a switchblade from his belt. The click of the opening blade came simultaneously with the arc of the man's arm.

Carter rolled and felt the hissing whisper of air as the blade flicked past his head. There was a thud, and the point chipped plaster from the opposite wall. The goon tried to push the table from in front of him and retrieve the knife.

The Killmaster himself lunged forward. He slammed the heels of both hands violently against the table edge and drove the flimsy top into the man's belly. When the upper torso and head flopped forward, Carter chopped the heels of both hands over the man's ears.

He screamed, and went down and out like a ruptured balloon.

Suddenly the hallway exploded. At the same time, the man's falling body shoved the table forward into Carter, spinning him away. As the Killmaster rolled around, he saw that the action had saved his life. From another door, a second of Poulson's henchmen had appeared. The Walther had barked twice. One slug had slammed into the wall in a direct line where Carter had been. The other had plowed into the skull of the already dead man.

The shooter was bringing the Walther around for another try when Carter lurched to his knees and drove his shoulder against the table and into the man's side. He heard rather than saw the man's gun fall to the floor.

Carter upended the table and used his shoulder again to slam the man behind it into the wall. When the table slid down, the man was squirming upward like a crippled snake.

Deftly, he yanked his cohort's knife from the wall and came at Carter.

But he was too late. The Killmaster flipped the table around, brought it high above his head, and smashed it into splinters over the man's head.

Panting heavily, he stood over the dead man, trying to focus his eyes on one of the fallen guns as the shredded piece of furniture dropped to the floor. He spotted the guns at last, filled his hands with both of them, and sprinted down the stairs.

Near the bottom he could see the lead car and Jacobs's van thundering up the cobbled drive. Out of the corners of both eyes he could see shooters coming around both sides of the house. They fired, and the fire was returned from the moving vehicles.

In a great room to his right, he saw Poulson and one of the big gorillas who had carried him to the attic room the night before.

Their eyes met at the same time.

The machine pistol in Poulson's hand sprayed the entryway in front of Carter, blocking his path. He guided the Walther in his left hand around the archway and emptied the clip into the room. There was a loud scream that turned into a gurgling death rattle, and then the dull thud of a body hitting the floor.

The lead car was around the arc of the drive now and heading back toward the gate. Abruptly it skidded to a halt, and two of Jacobs's men rolled from the sedan's rear doors to the first position in the grass. They had barely hit ground when the machine pistols in their hands started barking toward the sides of the house.

The van itself was twenty yards short of the arc, and Carter knew it couldn't stop. He had to get by Poulson.

"Franz Poulson?"

"*Ja,* you son of a bitch!"

"Let's make a deal. Call your hounds off."

"No deal!"

"Why not?"

"Because if you don't kill me, he will."

"You mean Copperhead? Do you know who he is, Poulson?"

"I told you—no, I don't. No deals. I'm going to kill you, you son of a bitch."

The last word was barely out of his mouth when, again, the hall and the other side of the wall above Carter's head splintered with slugs.

"Poulson!" Carter shouted. "I want to talk. Here's my gun. I'm going to step into the doorway. Let's talk."

Carter reached his arm around the doorway and flipped

the empty Walther into the room.

"All right?"

"All right," Poulson growled in reply. "Let me see you."

Carter knew he had only seconds after showing his vulnerable body in the middle of the hallway. He had already jacked a shell into the chamber of the Walther in his right hand. He held it at his hip, then lifted his left hand high above his head.

"Coming now," he said. "Don't fire."

"Come ahead," Poulson said.

Carter took a deep breath, and then two steps into the hallway. He turned to see Poulson crouched over the other man's body, the machine pistol lifted in front of his face with both hands. The side of his head was a bloody mess, and his blond hair was matted with a combination of blood and sweat. Evidently, one of Carter's random shots had almost gotten him.

Carter moved forward. He could see the man's fingers, hands, and forearms tensing on the machine pistol. He readied his own Walther at his side.

"You're dead, bastard," Poulson said, his heavy jaw splitting in a leering grin.

"Am I?" Carter replied.

He brought the Walther up from his hip, firing as fast as he could squeeze off the shots. The first one hit the gorilla's body. The second, third, fourth, and fifth stitched up Poulson's frame. The sixth caught him square in the middle of the face and spread his brains over the wall behind him.

Carter dropped the Walther and quickly frisked the body, just in case the man might have something of value on him.

Nothing.

Outside, the war was still going on, but diminishing. The van was parked directly in front of the door, with its

back open. A machine pistol barked from the dark opening, keeping the shooters at the left of the house occupied.
The two agents near the sedan were holding the others
down at the right side of the house.

Carter sprinted to the double front doors and flung them
both open. ''Marty!'' he screamed into the night.

The man's face appeared at the side window of the van.
''Here! Run for it!''

At the same time, the door opened and Jacobs's words
brought a new round of gunfire from his people.

Carter dropped into a crouch and did a running duck
walk to the rear of the van. Five feet short, he dived. His
chest hit the side of the seat, and Jacobs's hand gripping
his belt dragged him the rest of the way inside.

''Go!'' Jacobs cried.

The back doors of the van slammed closed and the
vehicle lurched forward. They passed the sedan, which
quickly gathered its own and followed them. In single file,
they careened through the gate, hit the concrete, and
turned back toward the ferry that would take them across
the lake.

Jacobs was half over Carter's body, shaking.

''Are you all right?'' the Killmaster asked.

''Yeah,'' the man replied. ''I'm just laughing. Sixteen
years in this outfit, and this is my first war.''

''Stick with me,'' Carter chuckled, ''and you'll get
used to it. What have we got?''

''A woman named Emma Dunmetz, complete with
address. AXE Main is digging everything up on her now.
We've got a unit over her like a blanket.''

''Good,'' Carter sighed. ''There's just one more
thing.''

''Name it.''

''Gimme a cigarette.''

THIRTEEN

Carter rubbed more redness into his eyes and studied the picture of Emma Dunmetz. It had been taken fifteen years earlier, when the woman had just turned twenty. It would look nothing like the Emma Dunmetz of today, but it was all they had dug up on the woman.

The photograph had been taken when Dunmetz was in the corps of the Stuttgart Ballet. She was in a leotard, and it was easy to see why she had forsaken the ballet for teaching.

Emma Dunmetz did not have the figure for classical ballet.

She was tall, with legs like scissors, but a bust and hips like a porno flick star. Her hair was long, raven black, and she had an angular face that, even at twenty, had lots of maturity lines.

Carter looked up from the picture as Marty Jacobs entered the room. They had brought him directly from Poulson's to the safe house. After assuring themselves that the woman was under tight surveillance, Carter and Jacobs had grabbed some sleep.

Now the sun was rising steadily on a Sunday morning, and over Berlin the bells called to the faithful.

"The picture's old, but it'll have to do," Carter said.

''What about background?''

Before Jacobs could reply, the radio monitor crackled to life.

''Unit One, this is Two. Anything in the rear?''

''Nothing, but there's movement behind the blinds in the upstairs windows.''

Jacobs grabbed the mike. ''Unit Two, this is Main.''

''Yeah, Marty.''

''You got the picture?''

''We do, but it doesn't look a hell of a lot like her now. She went out for cigarettes last night and mailed a letter. We got a good look at her.''

''Okay. Stay on the air. I want to know if an eyelash moves!''

''You got it.''

Jacobs replaced the mike and handed a thin manila file to Carter. ''The life and times of Emma Dunmetz. It ain't much, but, like the picture, it's all we've got.''

Carter flipped the folder open and speed-read through the three pages it contained. Then he read it again, slowly, digesting every detail.

Dunmetz was born in Stuttgart to a couple who had toiled for years in the Zeiss optical plant. Besides being an industrial center, Stuttgart sported the best ballet in Germany, as well as the state opera and a fine orchestra.

As a young, gangling girl, she had achieved some fame and success with the ballet. As she grew older, she maintained her proficiency, but her height and voluptuous figure had curtailed any further advancement in her career.

She had been married once, but it had ended in divorce after a year.

Other than Stuttgart being the birthplace of the philosopher Hegel, who in turn had inspired Marx and Engels, there was nothing in the file that would connect Emma Dunmetz to her East German neighbors or Moscow.

"Marty?"

"Yeah?"

"It's thin. According to this, she's lily white."

"I told you."

"Get the records people to check the Stuttgart Ballet. Find out if the troupe traveled to Eastern Europe, especially to Moscow, during her tenure."

"Will do."

Marty Jacobs went to work on the phone. Carter lit a fresh cigarette and carried his coffee out to the small terrace overlooking a garden in the rear of the house.

The gimmick to get to Copperhead through Franz Poulson had worked, but it had also backfired. Now they had a woman's name, and the woman had nothing to do with military liaison.

She couldn't be Copperhead.

Did she know who Copperhead was? Would she screw up and lead them to the mole? What would she surmise when she read the Sunday-morning papers and found out that Franz Poulson had been killed in a gangland-style shoot-out the night before?

Jim Wilson had reported in that morning. They were under the wall and less than a day from the bunker.

Steve Hardin and the AXE communications crew were on standby alert for the early part of that week. With any luck, by Tuesday—Wednesday at the latest—the lines leading from the telephone and computer terminus in the bunker would be feeding them a gold mine of information.

That is, if Copperhead didn't nip them in the bud before they got hooked up.

"Nick . . ."

"Yeah?" It was Jacobs, with a wide smile on his face.

"Maybe bingo."

"Talk to me."

"In those seven years, the Stuttgart Ballet performed twice in East Germany and three times in Moscow."

Carter sighed aloud and felt a lot of tension go out of his

body. "A young, impressionable girl . . . she could have been turned early."

"Maybe more so than we think," Jacobs replied. "Her father was jailed by the Nazis briefly in 1938, as a Bolshevik. Shortly after that, he was conscripted and sent to the Eastern front. He was captured by the Russians and not released until 1948."

Carter whistled and drank the remaining coffee in his cup. "Let's hope she doesn't detour from the party line in the next few days."

The radio came to life as the two men moved back into the room.

"Main! Hello, Main, this is Unit One! Are you there, Marty?"

Jacobs grabbed the mike and barked a reply. "This is Jacobs. Talk to me."

"The lady is moving."

"Have you got her?"

"Like fleas on a dog. She just hailed a taxi about two blocks from the studio. We're using a three-car switch. I'm positive she doesn't know we're a tail."

"Good enough. Come back up in three minutes. Carter and I are going mobile. We'll join you."

"Right, but I got to tell you something, Marty . . . we almost missed her."

"What are you talking about?"

"She came out the back way as a little old lady, dressed in the whole nine yards . . . black dress, gray wig, and veil."

Carter and Jacobs exchanged hard stares. The same thought was in both their minds.

Fox's little old lady in the restaurant who disappeared.

Emma Dunmetz passed a bill to the taxi driver and told him to wait. She used her bent, arthritic walk as she moved slowly down the path to the canopied gravesite.

The coffin was in place, as were the mourners she had

hired the previous afternoon. All five of them were older women dressed much like herself. No one other than the priest gave her a glance as she moved anonymously into their midst.

The coffin was open, and inside it lay the street derelict whom, two days before, Emma Dunmetz had transformed into Estelle Bachman.

Seconds later, an olive-green army staff car pulled up behind the taxi and three men emerged. Out of the corner of her eye, Emma identified Herman Bachman. He walked like a man in anguished pain, his head bowed, his shoulders slouched. His arms were crossed in front of his chest, and clutched beneath them was a Bible.

Twenty feet short of the grave, the two officers, dressed in civilian clothes, dropped off. Bachman continued to the gravesite and approached the priest.

The two men exchanged a few words in low tones, and Bachman dropped to one knee. The priest blessed him, and Bachman rose and turned toward the grave. There were tears flowing from his eyes and his upper body shook.

The man, Emma thought, *had missed his calling. He should have been an actor.*

The priest began his prayers for the dead, and the women around Emma began their paid-for sobbing.

Bachman's timing was sheer perfection. Just as the priest was about to finish his litany, the miner screamed his anguish and threw himself at the coffin. He embraced the corpse and showered the waxy face with kisses.

Everyone was stunned, shocked into stillness.

Finally, Emma stepped forward and grasped him by the shoulders.

"Let her go, son, let her go," Emma intoned in her aged, cracking voice. "She's in God's hands now."

"Momma . . . Momma!" he wailed.

Emma was eventually able to get the crying man to his feet. In so doing, the black shawl she wore slipped from her shoulders into the coffin. When Bachman was settled, she turned to the priest and nodded her veiled head for him to continue. Just before stepping back into her own place among the other women mourners, she bundled the shawl to her waist.

In its folds was the Bible.

"What the hell was that all about?"

"I'd like to know what the hell *all* of this is about," Carter replied, dropping a pair of binoculars from his eyes.

They were standing in the belfry of a chapel two hundred yards from the gravesite. Just beyond the two entrances to the cemetery, units One and Two awaited instructions.

Marty Jacobs's fingers were white where they clutched a walkie-talkie. "What shall I tell the boys?"

"Stay on her. That's all we can do. Is there an administrative office around here?"

"Yeah, right down there in that glen."

Carter put the field glasses back to his eyes. "That's a staff car. You recognize any of the three men?"

"No."

"They're breaking up."

Carter and Jacobs watched everyone disperse.

"Have Unit Two stay with the woman. Send Unit One after that staff car."

Jacobs relayed Carter's orders to the two units and then followed the Killmaster down the narrow stairwell from the belfry.

"What now?"

"We find out who the dear departed was."

In the next two hours, they had checked out the identity of the corpse and confronted a very nervous funeral home director. The man described Emma Dunmetz to a T when he got to the part of his story about the late Estelle Bachman's female attorney.

There was little doubt in Carter's mind as they left the

funeral home and returned to the car that they had witnessed some kind of an elaborate drop.

The next question was, who was the son, Ernest
Bachman?

That was answered the moment Jacobs got back on the
radio.

"Unit Two, this is Main."

"How goes it?"

"She's back in her studio—not a peep out of her."

"Were the boys able to get in?"

"Oh, yeah, with time to spare. Got a tap on the phone
and a bug in each room."

"Good going. Unit One?"

"One here, Marty. We followed the staff car to a
security compound at Tegelhof, but we couldn't get past
the gate."

"Jesus Christ," Carter rasped, "gimme that. Unit
One, this is Carter."

"Yes, sir."

"Are you still at the compound?"

"Yes, sir, right across the street. I'm staring right at the
gate."

"What's the number?"

"Twelve."

"Out," Carter hissed, and turned to Jacobs. "Number
Twelve is the security quarters for the workers on Crown
Prince."

"Shit. Copperhead *did* get somebody in!"

"Let's move," Carter growled.

Dieter Belsen was a big, beefy man who had spent
thirty of his fifty years in the BfV, West Germany's
counterintelligence unit.

He listened quietly, nodding now and then, as Nick
Carter brought him up to date on Copperhead and Crown
Prince.

"And that's about it. His name is Bachman, and his
mother, Estelle Bachman, has been dead for two years."

"I'm glad, Herr Carter, that you have decided to bring the BfV in on this at last."

Carter shrugged. "He's a German national. I want my ass covered, but at the same time I want whatever I can get out of him."

"And you have your people watching this woman?"

Carter nodded. "We think Bachman passed her the dope on the tunnel somehow at the funeral. Hopefully, she'll pass it on to Copperhead."

"Then let us go talk to Mr. Bachman."

It was a hundred-yard walk to the enclave of twenty or more trailers housing the Crown Prince workers. When they arrived at Herman Bachman's trailer, Carter didn't bother to knock. He just flung the door open and stepped inside.

"Herman Bachman?"

"*Ja?*" said the surprised man, leaping up.

"My name is Nick Carter. I am with American intelligence. This is Dieter Belsen, BfV."

"So? What do you want with me? I am in mourning. I just buried my poor mother a few hours ago."

"Your mother, Herr Bachman, was buried two years ago in Hamburg. You're under arrest for espionage."

They worked in one-hour shifts, with two-man teams, all through the night. Now dawn was breaking and Herman Bachman hadn't told them a thing.

"It's a pity. If we were on the other side of the wall, there are many methods we could use," Dieter Belsen said, rubbing his red-rimmed eyes.

"That's the price we pay for scruples," Carter said with a sigh. "But if the woman doesn't come through, you may have to turn your head for a while."

"Nick?" It was Marty Jacobs, elation splitting his face.

"Yeah?"

"Our lady's moving!"

FOURTEEN

Bernard Evers drummed his fingers on the table as he waited for the switchboard to put his call through. At last his secretary answered.

"Marilyn, it's me."

"Yes, Captain?"

"A bit of the flu or something. I won't be in today."

"All right, sir, I'll put it on the duty roster. Feel better soon."

"Thank you, dear. See you tomorrow."

"Yes, sir."

Evers replaced the phone, and finished a cup of coffee as he moved to the window.

His watcher was still there, bored but watching.

The captain rinsed out his cup and put his telephone on the answering machine.

The hall was clear. He locked the door and darted up the stairs to Dr. Emil Bondorf's apartment. Inside, he quickly stripped out of his clothes and sat before a brightly lit makeup mirror.

It took nearly a half hour to age his face and add a short Vandyke beard and gray-flecked mustache. A gray wig and blue contact lenses over his brown eyes completed the facial disguise.

Next came one of the carefully tailored and heavily padded suits. He chose a dark pin-stripe three-piece and a conservative tie.

One hour after Captain Bernard Evers left his apartment, Dr. Emil Bondorf emerged from the front of the building, medical bag in hand.

Across the street, John Byram shuffled quickly through the Polaroids that had been taken of all the building's tenants and their guests.

When he found the match, he jotted in his notebook: *Dr. Bondorf out at 8:05* A.M.

Byram glanced up at Evers's windows and flipped on his walkie-talkie.

"Base, this is Byram with Evers."

"Yeah, John, go ahead."

"Evers is still in, and late."

"Will check."

It was nearly five minutes before the walkie came back to life. "Byram?"

"Yeah?"

"Checked the duty roster. Evers called in with a flu bug this morning."

"Shit."

"That's the way it goes, John. Stay out of the sun."

John Byram made the call notation in his log and moved farther back into the hallway. He lit a cigarette and prepared himself mentally for a long, boring day.

They followed Emma Dunmetz in three-team relays on foot and by car. Her route seemed aimless and without a definite destination.

Jacobs and Carter stayed back in an unmarked Volvo, remaining in touch with the teams by radio.

"You think she spotted a tail?" Carter asked.

"Hard to say," Jacobs said with a shrug. "It's possible from the aimless moves, but if she has, she's not trying to shake them."

The woman had window-shopped, stopped for a light breakfast, and simply walked. Because of the size of the surveillance team, it had been possible to put a man or another woman into every one of the places where she stopped.

All of them reported that she had definitely not made a drop.

"Get a new update on all our possibles."

Jacobs got on the radio to AXE Main, while Carter slipped from the car and walked to a newsstand for cigarettes.

By the time the Killmaster returned to the car, Jacobs had the poop on each member of the liaison team.

"Fox, of course, is still in custody. All the others have reported in to work, except Captain Evers. He checked in sick early this morning with his secretary—a flu bug."

"Who's on his building?"

"John Byram."

"Has he confirmed?" Carter asked.

Jacobs nodded. "Hasn't moved all weekend, and not a peep this morning. Want some more of this awful coffee?"

Carter shook his head.

The radio came to life.

"Unit One, Two here. Subject just entered St. Mark's Cathedral. Have you got an available we haven't used yet?"

"Affirmative. Sheila's on her way in."

That would be Sheila Morgan, one of the four women they were using. She would follow Dunmetz into the church and observe her every move.

Even though his throat was raspy raw, he lit yet another cigarette. It was all he had to keep the edge off his nerves.

The wait seemed forever until the radio crackled again.

"She's out and moving again. Coming your way, One!"

"Got her!"

It was another ten minutes before Sheila Morgan got on the air with her report.

"Subject did the usual with the holy water, and waited for another woman to clear the confessional. She was about ten minutes in the confessional and then left. No verbal or physical contact with anyone."

Carter turned to Marty Jacobs with a perplexed frown on his face. "That confessional would be a great place to make the drop if her contact was the priest."

Jacobs grabbed the mike. "Sheila, Marty here."

"Yes, Marty."

"Get back in there and check out the priest."

"Will do."

Carter was already diving into the briefcase on the seat between them. St. Mark's Cathedral had jarred two pieces in his memory. He found the two reports he needed and quickly glanced through them.

"It smells," he growled. "Look at this."

Jacobs speed-read Emma Dunmetz's brief dossier, then looked back at Carter, his face a question mark.

"Her religion. She was born and raised a Lutheran. She might have converted, but I doubt it. And there's this . . ."

Carter held up the watcher's movement reports on Captain Bernard Evers and ran his finger down the stops.

"Evers is supposedly a Catholic, but even if he were extremely devout, four confessions in a week is a little much."

Jacobs was already reaching for the mike. "Unit One, let Two take over the Dunmetz woman. You get into the cathedral. Question everyone and go over that confessional booth with a fine-tooth comb!"

"We're moving."

Jacobs changed channels and barked into the mike again: "Byram! John Byram, this is Jacobs!"

"Yes, sir."

"The safety's off. Take your backup and get into that

building. I want to make sure Evers is in there, even if you
have to break the door down!''

"Yes, sir, right away.''

''C'mon,'' Carter said, climbing from the car. ''I want
to talk to Sheila in person!''

Bernard Evers left the cathedral, hugging his right arm
over the Bible in his inside coat pocket. He looked neither
right nor left as he crossed the street and walked straight
away from the square.

He didn't have to look. He knew they were there somewhere. The young blond woman with the obviously
American clothes had been the tip-off. If the clothes
hadn't told him, the way she had collared the priest when
he stepped from the confessional would have.

The foolish bitch, Dunmetz, had been too smug.
Somehow they had gotten to her and tailed her to the
cathedral. No one had made him as Dr. Emil Bondorf,
but there was a chance that his Evers cover would be blown
soon if they put Dunmetz in the cathedral and monitored
his visits.

He crossed over two blocks and approached the square
from a smaller street. Just short of the square itself, he sat
at an outdoor café and ordered coffee.

It was only a matter of minutes before he saw the cars
converge and the blond woman go back into the cathedral.
When the agent, Carter, arrived, Evers knew that a change
of plans was imperative.

He hailed a cab and ordered the driver to take him to
Tegelhof Airport. Once in Frankfurt it would be much
easier to slip into East Germany.

He would have to make the delivery in person.

The cathedral, the priest, and the other three people in
the pews were of no help.

Carter narrowed in on Sheila Morgan. ''Think, Sheila
. . . every movement, every face you can remember.

Give me the whole picture from the moment you entered.''

The woman was borrowed from CIA. She was well trained, but she had only two years of field experience. This was why Carter wanted every scrap of information in her head.

He would sift and analyze it.

"The two women were there, in the front pew. The old man was up there by the altar. The subject was coming up the aisle. I think she had just left the confessional.''

"And this other man . . .''

'Gray-haired, heavyset . . . mid-sixties. He was just going into the confessional. I sat there and waited five, maybe six minutes. One of the old women finished praying and came back to this pew. When the gray-haired man came out, the old woman went in. That's it. I left to report to One.''

"Nick . . .''

It was Jacobs, running toward Carter and Sheila Morgan on the steps of the cathedral. Carter didn't like the scowl on the man's face.

"Tell me.''

"It's Evers. Byram entered the apartment. It's empty.''

"Shit. Have you ordered a crew there?''

"Yeah. They've already arrived and have started to take the place apart.''

"Let's get over there!''

"Mr. Carter . . .''

It was Sheila Morgan tugging at the sleeve of his jacket.
"Yes?''

"There's one other thing. It's such an awful long shot I was afraid to mention it.''

"Spit it out!''

"The gray-haired man. All of us have been comparing the snaps of the suspects, and everybody around them, between shifts. I think I've seen this man before, but I can't remember which one of us had the picture.''

Carter whirled on Jacobs. "Marty, get all the watchers to Evers's apartment. Put someone at all the border crossings and airports. We still might have a chance to pick him up. Berlin's not that easy to get out of."

Carter grabbed Sheila's arm, and together they sprinted to a car.

A half hour later she was holding the Polaroid of Dr. Emil Bondorf in her shaking hand.

"This is him. I'm sure of it."

"Byram!" Carter snapped.

"Yes, sir?"

"Get enough copies of this made to go around, and get them spread to the airport and all the exits."

"Yes, sir."

"And what apartment is this doctor in?"

Byram's reply had barely left his lips before Carter was heading for the stairs.

They were everywhere, and most were not trying to hide it. Bernard Evers had spotted them while purchasing his ticket. He had even seen one young man look directly into his face and then down into the palm of his hand.

He could guess that in the man's palm was a snapshot of Captain Bernard Evers.

Since the man had quickly passed him over, he surmised that his alter identity, Dr. Emil Bondorf, was still clear.

But he took no chances. Instead of going into the departure lounge, he entered a nearby men's room and parked himself in a booth.

There he waited until the very last minute before heading for his plane. They were giving the last call for boarding as he walked down the ramp.

Emma Dunmetz spotted the woman first, halfway between the cathedral and her studio. She took evasive action, and then discovered the two men.

It was a surveillance team: one woman, two men.

Had they been on her all day? Had they witnessed the drop? Had Copperhead picked up the Bible? And if he had, was *he* under surveillance?

She darted into a restaurant, went through the main room, and ducked into the restroom.

Two minutes later, through the crack between the booth's door and the frame, she saw the woman enter. The woman glanced at Emma's feet and then went to the mirror.

Emma watched her open her purse and begin to freshen her makeup. She looked down at her hands. They were steady. She took another twenty seconds to go over the procedure and then emerged from the booth.

"Good morning," Emma said in German. "It is a beautiful morning and you are an overweight cow."

The woman thought fast, looked at her blankly, and managed what she hoped was an uncomprehending smile.

"I said, you are a fat cow."

"I'm sorry, I don't speak German."

"Oh? English?"

"I am an American," she replied, turning to face Emma.

Emma hit her twice on the side of the neck. The woman dropped like a limp rag. When she was safely stashed in one of the booths, Emma emerged from the rest room and paused in the semidarkness of the hall. One man was in the street outside; the other sat at the counter, listlessly drinking coffee.

She went deeper into the hall. Near the rear door was a bank of two phones.

Her call was answered on the first ring.

"Ja?"

"This is Dancer."

"Ja?"

"I have been made."

"Are you sure?"

"I am positive. They have me under surveillance now. Was Copperhead able to connect?"

"Yes, he checked in a half hour ago. He is going over for a personal delivery."

"I must go over myself. I am sure they are just waiting to arrest me."

There was a pause, as if the person on the other end of the line were conferring with someone else.

"Can you elude your surveillance?"

"Yes."

"Where are you?"

"A café on the Lietzenburgerstrasse."

"Can you be at the Steinplatz in a half hour?"

"Yes."

"Southwest corner, a tan Opel, two men in the front seat. Inquire about directions to the Schlosspark Theater. They will offer to drive you."

The line went dead. Emma hung up the phone, and turned around to face two male AXE agents. The short blond woman was behind them. Her eyes were glassy and she was rubbing her neck with a shaky hand.

But she was awake . . . awake enough to warn her two comrades.

"Emma Dunmetz?"

"Yes."

"You are under arrest."

"For what?"

"Espionage."

"Preposterous! Besides, I am a German national. You are American. You cannot arrest me!"

The second man gripped her free elbow and spoke in perfect German. "My name is Borst, Fräulein, and I am BfV. I assure you that you are under arrest."

It was a beautiful setup. Captain Bernard Evers was clever. He had managed to come over as a very deep mole, and until he was activated, he had built up his own position and created an alter identity as Dr. Emil Bondorf.

But now both of them were blown and could never be used again.

Phase one of three was completed.

Once this was established, and two teams were taking the apartment apart, Carter had no reason to remain. He and Marty Jacobs returned to AXE Main.

Both Hardin and Wilson had been summoned via the car radio, and were waiting.

Carter addressed Hardin first. "Are we hooked up?"

"We have been hooked up from the alternate tunnel for twelve hours and copying like hell."

Carter turned from Wilson to Hardin. The chase and the elaborate steup he had created was coming to an end. The Killmaster could feel the adrenaline of impending victory pumping through his body.

"Let's see the plans again. I want to go over every detail. When the times comes to go boom, we can't afford to be a second off."

Jim Wilson laid out a set of plans, smoothed them, and began to explain.

"Okay, here's the larger tunnel under the wall to the bunker we built with the imported crew. My people cut off right here with the second tunnel."

Carter scannd the map through a magnifying glass and smiled. He couldn't believe it had all gone so well.

"And you're sure, Steve, that there's no way they can detect the tap you put on the underground cable?"

"Positive," Hardin replied. "We used bypasses at three points, and at no time was there an interruption in their transmission."

Carter sighed. "Then the ploy of having them switch from an aboveground cable to an underground worked."

Hardin nodded. "Like a charm. There was no way we could have had the time aboveground to properly tap the topside cable. By tricking them into shifting it underground, it was a cinch."

"And the alternate tunnel has disappeared?"

"Completely," Wilson said, nodding. "We back-filled it and even packed it."

"So," Carter said with a chuckle, "when the time comes, they will know about the main tunnel, but not the alternate."

"I'd stake my reputation on it," Wilson said. "Particularly after the big one blows. That should wipe out any traces of the second dig."

" 'Should'?" Carter asked.

"Okay," Wilson said and smiled. "It *will* wipe out all traces of the smaller tunnel."

"Right. And you say your charges are ready against the wall of the bunker?"

"They go whenever you give the word," Wilson replied. "Care to let Jim and me in on all this now? I can understand the alternate tunnel, and the tap we made there. But why all the pretense of blowing the bunker when there's a one-hundred-percent chance the Vopos will be on our butts five minutes after we're through the wall?"

"For one thing," Carter replied, grinning broadly, "it will provide the perfect diversion from the smaller, filled-in tunnel."

"I can see that," Wilson said. "But, hell, we could have managed secrecy without going through the bunker wall."

"We could have," Carter admitted. "But, you see, once we're through the wall of that bunker, a couple of people are coming back our way with us. Now, where are the printouts of all the transmissions so far?"

"There, on the other desk," Hardin said.

"Good. You two get back to the tunnel, and send Jacobs in here."

The two engineers left, and Carter leafed through the computer printouts until he found the transmissions he sought. He had already gone through them once, and the analysis made of them by the special team they had brought in from Washington.

Now he went through them again just to make sure they had it all.

The Soviets had named their new laser research "Twilight." As research had guessed, they were very close to perfecting it. And the man who held the key was Adolph Grinsing.

Take out Grinsing and obtain his notes, and the West would be able to copy and perfect the system and a protection for their satellites.

With Grinsing terminated, the Soviets would have to start all over.

Marty Jacobs came through the door and paused at Carter's shoulder. "We picked up the Dunmetz woman."

"And?"

"They're interrogating her now. She's not exactly singing like a bird, but we think she'll come around when we offer her amnesty and exile to a Third-World country."

"If she talks, it will be just gravy. Have Klaus and Trena been contacted?"

"Yeah. They've been alerted to green light. All we have to do is give them the word when Copperhead is in place and he thinks he's won."

There was a knock on the door, and a young station clerk came in. "Marty . . ."

"Yeah?"

"They made Evers/Bondorf at the Frankfurt airport."

"Was he met?" Carter asked.

"No. He took a taxi, walked, and then took another cab. They followed by chopper and car. He ended up in a small schloss in the Taunus, north of Frankfurt, near Bad Nauheim."

"Do they have it nailed?" Carter asked.

"Yes, sir. Two teams."

"Have a jet ready for me in twenty minutes."

"Yes, sir."

The clerk left, and Carter noticed the scowl on Marty Jacobs's face. "You think that's wise?" the man asked. "Shouldn't we just let him fly?"

"No," the Killmaster replied. "I want him to believe all the way that we don't want him to go over with word on the tunnel. His information is gold to them, remember?"

"Yeah, but—"

"No, Marty. I want to make one more big play for him. I want him to be sure that the info he's bringing them on the main tunnel is worth everything to us."

"You're the boss."

"Besides, by doing it this way we get some more gravy."

"His Frankfurt network?"

"Right."

Both men stood, staring intently at each other for several seconds. The same thought was on both their minds.

"Green light?"

"Yeah," Carter smiled. "It's green light to Klaus and Trena all the way. Tell 'em Twilight Kill is on."

FIFTEEN

A misty, light rain had started to fall, the kind that has inspired poets to write about mountain mists for centuries. The higher they climbed into the mountains, the more pronounced it became.

The head of the surveillance team was Brian Carmichael, an old AXE hand that Carter had known for years.

Carmichael himself had picked Carter up at the Frankfurt airport. As they drove the fifteen or so miles north into the Taunus, the man briefed Carter on the situation.

"The schloss is hard to get to, but not impenetrable."

"How many are there besides our game?" Carter asked.

"An older couple, and a pair they claim are their sons. They are supposedly retired from an auto business in Zell in the Mosel valley. Evidently, they weren't too worried about background cover. One check and we were able to blow it."

Carter nodded. "They were probably on line just for Copperhead's use, no need to go too deep. Any dogs?"

"None, and according to the neighbors, no heavy artillery beyond a couple of hunting rifles. They probably didn't want the neighborhood to think they were creating a fortress.''

''Figures.''

The car rounded a curve and almost instantly they were in a small, picture-postcard village.

''This is Bad Nauheim. We climb from here. It's about four miles.''

Carter nodded and eased back into the seat with a sigh. It was almost over, only a matter of hours. And the only really tricky part was the one to be played by Klaus and Trena.

Trena.

Jesus, Carter thought, *I hope she makes it.*

Carmichael geared down and they started to climb. The going was slow, not only because of the fog and rain, but also because of chickens and squawking geese that darted across their path.

The mountain loomed in russet colors washed by the rain, and behind them the blur of Bad Nauheim was already disappearing in the mist and fog.

''There's a farmer's machine shed just above the schloss. We've set up shop there.''

''The farmer?''

''No sweat. The moment we said we were spy catchers, he gave us complete squatters' rights.''

''How are we on men?''

''Two teams of three each, mine and BfV. I mixed them up. And don't worry about the BfV boys. They're a crack team. I've worked with them before. Here we are.''

Carmichael pulled off the narrow road into an even narrower lane. They passed through a thick grove of trees and emerged into a muddy clearing. In its center was a small barn with a smaller shed attached.

There was a rather large pond just to the left of the barn. Geese glided across its surface, feeding.

''Nice, peaceful place,'' Carter mused.

"Yeah, isn't it. I told the farmer who owns it we'd try and keep it that way."

The two men left the car and walked toward the barn. Just short of the door, it opened and a rangy man with a no-nonsense look on his broad features stepped out to meet them.

"Nick, this is Bob Ferris, my second."

"Glad to meet you, Carter."

"Bob."

The two men shook hands and quickly appraised one another.

"Anything since I left?"

"Yeah," Ferris replied. "They brought a car in for him about an hour ago. Want to have a look?"

Carter nodded, and they moved through the barn and out by a second, rear door. Twenty feet beyond, the ground sheared off, straight down.

"That's the schloss, there to the right," Ferris said, handing Carter a pair of field glasses.

It was a turn-of-the-century copy, in miniature, of an old Rhineland castle. One round observation turret jutted above the roof with its many chimneys, and where there had been shooter holes in the walls of the original, there were now huge panes of glass.

The estate was fenced, and the lane winding a mile from the main road wasn't gated.

"No security," Carter grunted.

"I don't think they feel they need it," Carmichael said.

"I've got our people down there all ready to go," Ferris said. "All we need is the word."

"We'll wait until after dusk," the Killmaster replied. "Our pigeon won't want to run himself until after dark."

He put the glasses back to his eyes and scanned the courtyard in front of the house. There were three cars: a gray Mercedes, a white Volvo, and an older model American-built station wagon.

"Which car did they bring in for Evers?"

"The Volvo. Can't tell for sure, but it looks like it's got a rotary on the license plates. He can probably change them from inside if he picks up a tail."

Carter smiled. "He'll have a tail, all right. Where's mine?"

"There, in the trees across the main road."

"Good," Carter said, dropping the glasses and facing the two men. "You gave your people the word?"

Carmichael nodded. "We did."

"It has to be that way, huh?" Ferris added.

"It does," Carter replied.

"The bastard. I'd like to waste him nice and slow with a hunting knife, peel him inch by inch."

"We all would," Carter said. "But what he's taking over is going to do us more good than it is them. He has to make it."

Both men shrugged, but nodded in agreement.

"We've got sandwiches and coffee in the barn."

"Good," Carter said. "I could use some food and a catnap. It will be dark in about an hour. We'll go shortly after."

They were spaced around the schloss like Indians ringing a wagon train. Carter had taken the front himself, more to make sure that one of the others didn't get trigger-happy and drop Evers when he—they hoped—ran from the house.

Fifteen minutes earlier he had checked out the dark blue Opel he would use for the chase car. Now he was about three hundred yards in front of the house, crouched in some bushes.

There were several rooms lighted in the schloss, the glow exaggerated by the fog. He checked the loads in Wilhelmina, then squinted his eyes on a spot in the forest about two hundred yards above the schloss.

Three minutes later he saw the flash: three quick spurts of light and then one long one.

It was a go.

He moved out fast, jogging over a small wooden bridge and then taking a sharp right. The trees were thick and tall, allowing him to stick to the lane. As he moved through them, he was aware of the piney smell of the woods and the sharp freshness of the altitude. It cleared his lungs and his head.

There was one more turn. He caught a glimpse of rushing white water and heard the sound of it tumbling over rocks.

Over the second bridge, he gained the end of the trees and the edge of the courtyard.

Up close, the schloss was even more portentous and wrapped in gloom.

It was twenty yards to the nearest car, the Mercedes. Ten yards beyond that was Evers's Volvo.

Carter cleared the whole distance in seconds and rolled under the Volvo's rear bumper. He quickly attached the beeper and rolled on to the old station wagon.

When the air had been let from the two outside tires, he darted back around the Volvo to the Mercedes. Hugo made short work of two tires, and the Killmaster sprinted back to the protection of the woods and fog.

Pulling a flashlight from his pocket, he shot three shorts and a long toward the mountain. As he discarded the flashlight, he could almost sense the movement of the black-clad men down through the trees.

It seemed to take forever. He listened to the drip of water from the pungent pines, the more distant rush of the brook running down the mountain, and the harsh rasp of his own breathing.

Then the first shot was fired, followed by several more from the rear. He could see dark figures on both the right and left of the house, charging.

There was the clatter of broken glass, and then more firing. Suddenly a pair of French doors flew open on the third floor, and a figure backed out onto the balcony.

He held a barking machine pistol in his hands, firing wildly back into the room he had just vacated.

Suddenly the muzzle of the machine pistol flew upward. It continued to fire, the slugs stitching along the side of the building, spewing chips from the brick.

Then it was silent and the man was falling over backward. He seemed suspended in the room's light for several seconds, and then down he came to land with a dull thud in the cobbled courtyard.

"Come on, come on!" Carter hissed.

As if in answer to his words, the large oak door flew open and a man stepped through it. He turned, and for a brief second before the man loosed two shots from the pistol in his hands, he was brightly illuminated by the foyer light.

It was Captain Bernard Evers.

There was an answering hail of slugs from somewhere deep in the house. None of them caught Evers, but he was showered with splinters from the shattered doorjamb.

That was enough.

He whirled and practically threw himself down the steps. In seconds he was in the Volvo, and the powerful engine was roaring to life.

Carter waited until the car had lurched around and the headlights came on before he charged out of the trees.

The tires screamed on the cobbles as Evers floored the machine, spinning it around until it was in line with the mouth of the lane.

And then it was careening forward, with Carter running full tilt to intercept.

The Killmaster beat the Volvo by a full forty yards to the mouth of the lane. He stopped, raising his Luger, as the car hurtled toward him. But he didn't fire.

He waited just long enough in the glare of the headlights to make sure that Evers recognized him.

Then he jumped and rolled.

Evers swerved in an attempt to grind him under the left

front wheel. But Carter had rolled into the trees, and rather than jeopardize his own escape by curling a fender into a tire, Evers righted the car and sailed on.

He was barely past, when Carter jumped to his feet and gained the center of the lane.

He emptied the Luger into the trunk, being careful that no shot went high enough to ricochet through the glass and make a hit.

When the Volvo's taillights had disappeared, Carter jacked a fresh magazine into Wilhelmina's butt and walked slowly to the Opel.

He started the engine and switched on the receiver. After thirty seconds to warm up, the small gold ball against the green background became clear. It moved steadily down the mountain.

After activating his own beeper so Carmichael could follow him, Carter pulled out and began to follow.

He had a pretty good hunch at the isolated spot where Evers would cross into East Germany. He also had already picked out a place where he would try and fail one last time to intercept the man.

Evers stayed off the autobahn, taking back roads toward the Gottingen crossing. Another half hour and he would be over. Three hours beyond that and he would be decoding the Bible in East Berlin.

That white Opel was behind him again. Or was it the same one? Opel did make more than one white sedan. But still . . .

Ahead of him, the highway wound like a dark gray ribbon through the trees. He passed through villages without slackening his speed.

Twenty minutes to the frontier.

Evers glanced into the rearview mirror.

The Opel was back.

He accelerated around a curve, and the big 550's engine keened doing what it did best.

Evers, despite his concentration on the physical process of driving at night at great speed, began to sweat and watch the headlights behind him more and more.

Ahead was a bad curve, sharp and dropping steeply on the other side.

On the flat stretch approaching the curve, Evers eased off on the gas pedal. Behind him he could see the Opel closing in fast.

Suddenly the smaller car was hovering off his left rear quarter. Defensively, he swerved the Volvo into the left lane, and then he realized that that was exactly what the other driver had wanted him to do. With a warbling of tires, the Opel bobbed full to the right and pulled up alongside. Evers saw no gun, but he heard the crack in the air and the sun visor buckled and stung his face with a spattering of debris.

The bastard was shooting at him.

Evers hit the brake lightly and got far enough behind the other car to see the driver in his lights.

Carter. It's that son of a bitch Carter.

But how?

And then he saw the green glow on the other driver's face, and realized. The bastard had put a beeper somewhere on the Volvo.

The curve was coming up fast now. Carter had slowed until he was abreast of the Volvo.

The fool, Evers thought, *the bloody, fucking fool!*

Just short of the curve and the steep precipice beyond it, Evers braked hard. The Opel shot by him. It had barely cleared his front fender when Evers geared down and floored the big car.

He smacked the right side of the Opel with the driver's side of the Volvo. When he was sure the driver's side of the Opel was mashed securely against the guardrail, Evers applied more pressure by veering left and speeding up.

He would have liked to see the fear on Carter's face as the Volvo forced him against the fence, but he didn't dare turn from the road for fear he would go over himself.

Side by side, sparks flying where they met, the two cars careened around the curve.

"So long, bastard!" Evers screamed with glee as he felt the weight of the Opel leave the Volvo.

And then the guardrail gave and the Opel started over.

Evers regained the center of the road and glanced up once in the rearview to see the Opel teeter and then plunge down the side of the mountain.

"Good riddance, you son of a bitch," he chortled, and applied more gas to the Mercedes.

It was only five more minutes to the frontier.

Carter lay in the arc of the curve where he had stopped rolling. His timing had been perfect. Another five seconds and he would not have had the road's shoulder to land on.

He waited until the red lights of the Volvo had diminished far enough so he could be sure Evers wouldn't see his silhouette when he stood.

Far below him at the base of the mountain, the Opel burst into flames.

"So long, bastard," Carter said, and lit a cigarette.

Carmichael found him like that fifteen minutes later, leaning calmly against the guardrail and smoking another cigarette.

"I guess it went all right?"

"Absolutely perfect," the Killmaster replied, flipping the butt away and climbing into the car. "He bought it all. I imagine he's already fitting the medal on his chest. No, Carmichael, Bernard Evers has no doubts that we wanted him dead and the info he's got squelched."

"Great. Where to now?"

"The airport. I've got a date in a tunnel."

SIXTEEN

No cars were parked along the narrow street. Klaus Klassen pulled the Ziv sedan to a halt and killed the engine.

"Which house?" Trena murmured.

"That one," her brother answered, pointing to a narrow two-story brick structure behind a high hedge about thirty yards off the street.

One upstairs window was illuminated. Its light peeked at them through the foliage of shrubs and young trees.

"A well-tended neighborhood."

Klaus chuckled. "Herr Dr. Adolph Grinsing is a genius, my little sister, a darling of the state."

"Are you sure you don't want me to go in with you?"

"I'm sure."

"Klaus . . ."

"No," he hissed, sliding from the car and silently closing the door behind him. "They might ask both of us for credentials, and needless to say yours would appear strange with the ruse I'm going to use."

He moved around to her side of the car and, with his back to the house, checked the loads in a Walther. Satisfied, he screwed a short-barreled silencer into the Walther's barrel and slipped it back into the holster under his left armpit.

"Check your own piece, Trena. If a Vopo patrol comes along and you can't talk your way out . . . shoot your way out."

Trina nodded. "Klaus . . ."

"*Ja?*"

"Good luck."

He leaned through the window and kissed her on the cheek. "We make our own good luck, remember?"

He turned, squared his shoulders, and walked through the open gate. Above him the red tiles of the houses' roofs gleamed wet with the rain. Beneath his feet were puddles.

Klassen ignored them, walking through the water rather than avoiding it.

The iron door knocker was in the shape of a fist. Klassen raised it and then let it drop with a dull thud.

A light popped on through an open door in the rear of the hall. Seconds later a short, thin man in shirt-sleeves with an open collar appeared.

Klassen watched him approach with a pistol held at his side near his hip.

"*Ja?*" the man asked through a speaker slot in the door.

"Klassen, Vopo Security. We have a tip that the doctor may be in danger. Supposedly, two men have come over from the other side."

"You have credentials?"

"*Ja.*"

Klassen held his police identity card up to the slot. The hall light came on, and then he heard the double locks of the door opening.

"I will tell Herr Doktor you are here."

"Are you armed?" Klassen asked.

"*Ja.*" The man held up his pistol.

"Good. I would like to check the rear garden before I talk to Herr Grinsing."

The man shrugged and stepped out onto the steps.
"This way."

Klassen followed the man to the corner of the house and
around. "Do you have any security in the house?"

"*Nein.* Leo lives in the guesthouse there. We can call
him if there is any trouble. He is assigned by state security
to the doctor."

Klassen spotted the small guesthouse. It appeared to be
a one-room studio.

They were just passing a water fountain spewing rip-
pling water from spigots from its top.

"Should I call Leo?"

"Don't bother," Klassen replied. "I'll do it."

He raised the silenced Walther and halted it three inches
from the back of the man's head. He fired twice.

Only one shot was needed. The first slug tore through
the man's skull and took the top of his head with it.

The man flopped forward, what was left of his head
lolling in the pool at the base of the fountain.

Klassen watched a thick line of blood rise in the water
and float across the pool, then he walked to the guesthouse.

"Leo?"

A groaned reply came through the door, the kind that
comes from a man who has been jerked to partial wakeful-
ness.

"Leo!"

"*Ja, ja* . . . who's there?"

"Vopo Security . . . get out here at once!"

There was the thud of feet hitting the floor, and then a
heavy tread. The moonlight was behind Klassen, bathing
the door when it was jerked open.

"What the hell . . .?"

The first slug hit him dead center in the chest. He was
lifted off his feet and flung backward into the small room.

Klassen followed him. As Leo spit blood and tried to
rise, the Vopo officer fired a second round directly into the

middle of his forehead.

As a safety measure, he jacked a fresh magazine into the Walther as he walked back to the front of the house. At the corner he holstered the gun.

The door was still ajar, and now there were several lights on in the upstairs rooms.

A tall, paunchy, gray-haired man in a robe and slippers was halfway down the stairs when Klassen stepped through the door.

"Who are you? Where is Boris?" As he spoke he lifted a short-barreled .38 and pointed it at Klassen's gut.

"Your man and Leo are searching the grounds, mein Herr."

"And you?" The gun didn't waver.

"Vopo Security . . . counterespionage." Klassen handed over his identity card. "You are Dr. Grinsing?"

"*Ja, ja,* I am Adolph Grinsing," the old man growled in reply, studying the card through thick glasses. "What is this all about at this hour of the night?"

The pistol in his hand lowered slightly when he handed the card back.

"We have information that two men came over this evening, Herr Grinsing, for the specific purpose of assassinating you and burglarizing your house."

"*Mein Gott . . .*"

"No fear, Doctor, I have patrols at both ends of the street, and I have alerted your man and Leo. However, it might be wise to check anything of value in the house."

"The only thing . . . *mein Gott . . .*"

Suddenly the gun in the man's hand was forgotten. He bounded down the rest of the stairs with surprising agility for a man of his years. Past Klassen he went, and on down the hall. At the last door on the left, he turned.

Klassen followed him, drawing the Walther and holding it at his side.

It was the living room, high-beamed and oak paneled.

Grinsing went right to the far wall and a large painting.

He shoved the painting aside to reveal a safe behind it.

Klassen waited patiently when the other man fumbled with the dials and finally yanked the door open. In his haste he had set the .38 down on a table by his side.

As Grinsing reached into the safe with both arms, Klassen moved the gun out of reach.

"Ach, they are safe. These are the only things of value that I have."

"And what might those be?" Klassen asked innocently.

"My notebooks."

"Thank you, Doctor."

Klassen raised the Walther in a practiced, fluid motion and shot him in back of the right ear.

The body crumpled and the notebooks fell at Klassen's feet. There were three of them. He quickly picked them up and, without bothering to look at their contents—he wouldn't have understood the contents anyway—started methodically through the house.

In every room he shut off the lights. Back in the foyer, he took one last look, shut off that light, and stepped outside. He clicked the lock, pulled the door shut, and walked briskly down the drive to the front walk.

There was no auto or pedestrian movement on the street either way as far as he could see.

"The notebooks," Trena said with obvious relief as Klassen slid into the car.

"Three of them. Let's hope they are the right ones."

"Even if they are," she replied, sliding them into a briefcase on her lap, "Moscow can't go much further on Twilight without Grinsing. I assume he is . . ."

"He is . . . very."

Klaus Klassen checked his watch as he started the Ziv. It was eleven-ten.

They had fifty minutes to get to the communications terminus and into the bunker.

● ● ●

Hardin and Wilson led the way, with Carter close behind them. Trailing the rear was the explosives expert, Nate Levine. As they moved, Levine carefully instructed his three-man crew on the trail of charges they were laying.

The tunnel was high enough for a tall man to move through easily in a bit of a crouch. The width was comfortable for two men abreast.

"How much will go when you blow those?" Carter asked.

"Right down the middle, give or take a few feet either way," Levine replied with a chuckle. "I put it a few feet on our side, just in case. After all, I wouldn't want to crumble their precious wall."

Carter nodded and moved on under the string of low-watt bulbs that provided illumination. Eventually he came out into the end of the tunnel. It was a space about nine by nine, and better lit than the tunnel itself.

Hardin and Wilson were waiting for him. Wilson spoke.

"Nate has explained the principle of these charges to me. Want to hear it?"

"You bet your ass I do," Carter replied. "Especially if I'm going right in after it."

"Okay. If our info is correct, the wall of the bunker is only about two feet thick here. He's placed four charges—here, here, here, and here—in a diamond shape."

"How much stuff?" Carter asked.

"He tells me enough to blow a good-sized hole in concrete twice that thick."

"And we're only going to be back there twenty feet?"

Wilson laughed. "Don't worry. Nate's never missed yet."

"Is that why he's only got two fingers on his left hand?"

Hardin shrugged. "One slight miss."

Wilson continued. "These are six-inch-thick blast directional shields. We've drilled into the bunker wall to anchor them, then recemented after their steel legs were in place. Besides the shields directing the force of the blasts, Nate is using a special plastique. It's cored so it is itself somewhat directional."

"It's the same explosive a lot of demolition experts use to implode buildings."

"What's their chance of survival on the other side?" Carter asked.

"One hundred percent," Nate Levine answered, moving into the larger area with a handful of detonator wires and clips. "That is, if they do what they've been told."

He moved to the wall and began attaching the detonator clips to the four corners of the diamonds. As he worked he finished the explanation, throwing words in an offhand manner over his shoulder.

"If our poop's right, there's an equipment storage room on the other side of this wall. If your people stick precisely to the time schedule, there shouldn't be any problem."

Carter gazed at the center of the diamond with squinting eyes. He tried to imagine the other side of the two-foot-thick concrete wall.

Electronic repair equipment, including large cable spools stored in the large, low-ceilinged room.

One door, steel, located directly across from the middle of the diamond where the full force of the blast would be.

The timing would have to be absolutely precise.

After gaining access to the bunker, Trena and Klaus Klassen would have to make their way through the generator and cable rooms to the steel door of the storage room.

Once there, they would have to wait until twelve midnight, sharp, before opening the door. If they were ten seconds early, or the blast was ten seconds late, they might be in the room when the wall blew.

"How much will we feel on this side?" Carter asked.

"A small shock wave at the most," Levine replied.

"And on the other side?"

"Demolition derby," Levine said. "There, that's it. How much time have we got?"

"It's eleven-thirty," Carter replied. "We've got a half hour."

SEVENTEEN

The building on Unter den Linden was gray and grim, as were the two men in a small cubicle on the sixth floor. At this time of the evening, the Office of State Security was usually quiet, the parking lot at the rear vacant.

Not this evening.

Bernard Evers had put a twenty-man squad on alert in the event that Bachman's Bible revealed a situation that needed to be handled at once.

A black, Russian-built Volga, two Ziv sedans, and a BTR-60 eight-wheeled armored personnel carrier stood ready to move at Evers's command.

Upstairs, Evers himself paced. Now and then he would glance at the small man with the mouse-colored hair who bent so diligently over the Bible and a cipher book.

The man's name was Gregor. He was a crypto specialist, and as far as Evers was concerned, he was going far too slowly.

"What is taking so damned long?" Evers suddenly blurted in exasperation, stopping directly behind the man.

"I'm sorry, mein Herr, but the keys that Herr Bachman engraved on the Bible's cover are not very deep. Some of the symbols I am only getting by trial and error."

Evers grunted, refilled his coffee cup, and stomped to the window.

Below, he could see the men milling in the courtyard, angry that they had been called from their barracks for no apparent reason. The personnel carrier's commander stood in the hatch behind the machine gun turret, smoking. Now and then he would glance up at the lighted window with a scowl on his face.

Evers prayed that he would have use for these men this night.

There was little doubt now that his cover was blown. Years of painstaking work building such a cover, and now it was gone.

Moscow would be very displeased if he had blown it for less than a very, very important reason.

Worse yet, Emma Dunmetz, the best courier in West Berlin, had been captured and his cell in Frankfurt taken out.

Yes, tonight would tell the tale, Evers thought. Either he would be a hero who could look forward to a soft job and a good pension, or he would be disgraced.

"Herr Evers, I have it!"

Evers whirled just as the man, Gregor, punched the printer button on his computer. At once, the American-made machine began to clatter.

Evers bent over it, reading as the paper scrolled up.

"Jesus Christ, they are tunneling under the wall, right into the bunker at Alderstaadt! Get me a track map, hurry!"

"*Ja, mein Herr*. Right away."

The little man scurried from the room. Evers tore the sheet from the computer as soon as the directional coordinates appeared, and studied them intently until the man returned.

"Here is a map of the Alderstaadt track for the area on both sides of the wall."

Evers ripped the map from the man's hand and spread it on a nearby table under a pool of light.

Quickly he traced the coordinates until he had the direction under the wall and the exact spot where they planned on breaching the bunker.

Then he laughed.

"With any luck, we'll bury them in their own tunnel!" He whirled on the man. "Get a complete copy of this to Central here in Berlin, and send another to Moscow at once!"

Without waiting for an answer, Evers bolted for the door and the stairs.

It was eleven-forty.

Klaus Klassen drove as fast as he dared through the quiet village of Alderstaadt. As he neared the area of the bunker, a black Chaika with two uniformed Vopos in the front seat passed him.

"We'll be in the forbidden zone in another block," Trena whispered.

"I know. Damn!"

The Chaika stopped directly in front of them, and both Vopos got out.

"What shall we do?" Trena murmured, her hand already creeping into the briefcase on her lap as if anticipating her brother's thoughts.

"We don't have time to talk our way through."

The Walther was already out of its holster and in the darkness by the car door. Trena's pistol hovered in her left hand behind the lid of the briefcase.

They rolled down their respective windows as the two Vopos approached, thankfully one on each side of the car.

"*Guten Abend, mein Herr.*"

"*Guten Abend.*"

"Do you realize that you are entering the forbidden zone right across the street?"

"I am Colonel Klassen, Central Security," Klassen said evenly.

"I am sorry, Colonel, you will have to turn around. No one is—"

"Now!" Klassen growled.

Both guns made their champagne-cork-popping sounds at once.

The Vopos staggered back, their hands clutching their chests, blood seeping through the webs of their fingers.

"Again!" Klassen barked, aiming carefully at his man's heart and firing a second time.

His sister didn't need to be told. She had already leaned far out of the window and pumped a second slug into the side of her prey's head.

"How much time?" Klassen asked, tromping the accelerator.

"Ten minutes. It's eleven-fifty."

Nate Levine did a last-minute check on the four wall charges and tested his power.

It was go.

"Okay, everybody back!"

They all moved back into the tunnel to the place, about thirty yards from the room, that had been previously designated.

Carter checked the safety of the machine pistol he held and heard the others around him doing the same.

Levine was right in front of him, closing an improvised shield that had been built into the shoring on the sides of the tunnel.

"Everybody got their goggles on?" Levine shouted.

There was a chorus of yesses.

"Okay," Carter said. "We go with the blast, right through the smoke and cement dust."

"How many minutes?"

"Nine."

● ● ●

The Vopo guard at the fence gate read and reread Klassen's identity card in the glow of a flashlight in his hand.

"I don't know, Colonel. Your name is not on the authorization list."

"I told you, dammit, this is an emergency security check! We have reason to believe the wall has been breached near here!" Klassen blustered, watching the man carefully.

The guard was a slave to authority, and a Vopo colonel was definitely authority. But he also had standing orders that no one was to be admitted to the bunker.

Klassen explained the situation to him again, urging all the authority he could muster into his voice.

At last the guard shrugged and turned to Trena. "Very well, but I will have to see your papers as well, Fräulein."

Klassen raised the Walther and shot the man in the back of the head.

"Come on!"

"Oh, my God . . ."

Klassen whirled. Coming around the corner were a line of official cars and a personnel carrier. Suddenly the spotlight on the carrier's turret came on, bathing them and the dead guard in stark white light.

A megaphone blared in the otherwise still night air:

"Stay where you are!"

Klassen raised the Walther in both hands, steadied it, and shot out the light.

"Run!"

Crouching low, they both ran toward the single entrance to the bunker.

"Halt right where you are!"

The blaring voice from the megaphone had alerted two more guards inside. They burst through the door, unslinging their machine pistols as they moved.

Like the well-trained team they were, Trena took on the one on her side, her brother the other.

Together they leaped over the bodies and burst through the door.

At the bottom of the first flight of stairs, another guard sat at a table, reading.

He looked up, gasped, and started to rise just as Trena shot him.

At the bottom of the second flight of stairs, they paused to get their bearings.

The hum of a powerful generator to their left told them where to go.

They burst through the generator room and on into the huge room where miles of cable lined the walls and ceiling.

Klassen stopped just long enough to close and lock the door behind him before they ran across the room to crouch behind the second steel door.

"The equipment storage room is on the other side of this door. How much time?"

"None," Trena replied. "It's midnight."

The words had barely left her mouth when they heard keys being inserted into the door they had just locked.

Simultaneously, the room seemed to shake, and from the other side of the door they were crouching against came a long, sustained roar.

"Go!" Carter yelled, lurching forward through the smoke and dust.

He could feel and sense the charging bodies at his side and behind him, the lights on their miner's hats piercing the gray cloud in front of them.

By twos they dived through the gaping hole that had once been the center of the diamond.

"Shit!" Carter screamed.

As one, they all saw the problem at the same time.

The blast had thrown some of the stored equipment in the room against the far door. Worse yet, the door opened *toward* them instead of back into the room where Klaus and Trena Klassen were waiting.

"Quick!" Carter barked. "Everybody on it!"

Letting their machine pistols rock from their slings at their sides, the men tore at the equipment, scattering it to the side. It was a superhuman effort, with each man suddenly strengthened to three times his normal power from sheer fear and need.

At last the door was cleared. Carter yanked it open just as the door of the adjoining room across from them was also opened.

"Get back, everybody!" Carter shouted, dropping to one knee and raising his machine pistol.

Trena and Klassen practically dived over him into the safety of the equipment room. As startled men appeared in the opposite door, Carter opened fire. Just above his left and right shoulders, Hardin and Wilson did the same.

The first five men through the door formed a pile in a slick of their own blood. When the doorway was practically blocked with bodies, Carter and the others began to fall back, inch by inch, still firing. When they reached the wall of the bunker, Carter shouted over the din:

"Get through!"

Hardin, then Wilson, dived through the hole. Carter followed, and the three of them ran as fast as they could to join the others in the tunnel.

Ahead they could see Nate Levine's grinning face, his hands steady on the black detonator control box.

Carter slid to a halt, then crouched beside Levine.

"Wait until they're deep in." He paused, throwing a grin up at Klaus Klassen. "I spotted Copperhead just before we went through the wall."

"We get him after all," Klassen said, matching Carter's almost gleeful expression.

"We do indeed."

"The sensors are hopping all over the place," Nate Levine growled.

"Where are they?" Carter asked.

"Just short of the halfway point."

"Can they dig out from there?" Carter said.

Nate Levine chuckled. "Maybe . . . in a few hundred years."

"Blow 'em to hell!"

Instantly, the ground around them shook and a deafening roar came to their ears. The tunnel far in front of them collapsed. There was no dust or smoke this time, only the dull glow of a single remaining bulb illuminating tons of earth.

Carter stood. Trena was at his side. He slid an arm around her waist, and with one finger tilted her chin upward.

"Just another day at the office," he said.

"The last day, for a while, I hope," she replied with a smile. "I think it's about vacation time."

"I agree. Just as soon as we check the recorders. Our little alternate line may be feeding us a whole new assignment."

DON'T MISS THE NEXT NEW
NICK CARTER SPY THRILLER

THE SAMURAI KILL

Fukoa returned and reported that Madame Ashekagi would see Carter and Siobhan as Mr. Takeda wished. Takeda left, and Fukoa seemed to brighten at once, to turn into a different man—brisk, in charge.

"A boat is at the dock now if you are ready."

They followed Fukoa back to the dock and rode across the Ariakeno-umi. At the village dock Dr. Fukoa took them to a small Honda sedan. The home of the Ashekagi family was a large Japanese-style house with an outer courtyard entered through a solid gate in a street wall. Fukoa rang and a servant in a kimono opened the outer door and ushered them into the courtyard.

As the gate closed behind them, seven men in black kimonos, wearing white headbands emblazoned with red characters, a pair of samurai swords thrust into their sashes, appeared all around Carter, Siobhan, and Fukoa.

"What . . . what . . . do you . . . ?" Fukoa stammered, stepping toward the tallest of the men in the black kimonos.

The long sword seemed to shine in the afternoon sun without even being drawn, without the swordsman seeming to move. The long sword, a *katana,* in his hand as if by magic, sliced through the air, its end pointed high into the sky, silver and dripping red as Fukoa's head fell to the dirt of the courtyard while his body stood for a second longer before falling beside it.

Wilhelmina cut down the sword-wielding warrior in the black kimono and red-lettered headband who leaped at Carter.

Siobhan had her small Walther PPK. She shot the swordsman attacking her. But the black-garbed man grunted, scowled, and kept coming on toward her.

A second man was on Carter with incredible speed, the shining arc of the *katana* aimed at Carter's neck. Carter went in under the hiss of the sword. The swordsman kicked Wilhelmina from his hand. From his crouch, Carter chopped the swordsman's supporting leg, sending him crashing to the courtyard dirt. Rolling, the man drew his *wakizashi* short sword and came up in a single motion. Carter snatched the long *katana* from the hand of the man he'd shot dead.

Siobhan shot again. The attacker grunted again, his sword sweeping so close under her chin she fell backward to the dirt, her Walther knocked from her hand. With a savage cry the wounded man closed in, hurled himself at her with his failing strength, and flew over her head as she caught his chest with both feet and flung him over her, his sword driving into the dirt of the courtyard, his body hanging from the hilt more dead than alive.

Charging, the attacker with the *wakizashi* parried Carter's lethal slash of his borrowed sword, ducked under, and came up in a liquid flow with the short sword plunging toward Carter's heart. Carter spun, dropping him with a high kick to the chin, the neck snapping so loudly, it echoed through the courtyard.

The four remaining attackers pressed in.

Siobhan grabbed a long *katana*.

They faced, four against two.

The tall leader who had killed Dr. Fukoa spoke sharply to his men in Japanese, assuming that the Caucasians would not understand him.

"Full battle tactics! These two are trained with guns and swords. Kill or die for the honor of Fujiwara. Go!"

The four spread out, two facing Carter and two now advancing on Siobhan. The tall leader himself moved slowly toward Carter as if he had decided on the most dangerous adversary, the place of greatest honor. Carter smiled, and focused not on the man's hands but his feet.

"It is an honor to face the Fujiwara," Carter said in Japanese.

The tall leader answered in English. "So? You speak Japanese and know of the great Fujiwara clan. Perhaps it will not be without honor to kill you."

"A samurai who fights for a clan of courtiers has little honor to defend," Carter said, watching the second man inch to his left, the other two moving slowly to take Siobhan from two sides.

The tall leader's face darkened. "The Fujiwara are now samurai! The greatest family of the ancients is now the greatest family of the future! The clan that will renew the blood of Japan, of the world!"

The second man was almost level with Carter now, between Carter and Siobhan. The two stalking Siobhan moved in ever closer to where she waited with the samurai sword resting on her shoulder like nothing more deadly than a garden tool. Only the tall leader had not moved, momentarily distracted by Carter's taunting.

"By killing unarmed scientists?" Carter laughed.

''The act of a peasant!''

The tall leader smiled. ''A feeble attempt to provoke me, American. You have studied—''

The second man's jaw muscles tensed to make his move. Carter swung his sword up and feinted a lunge at the tall leader. The second man saw his chance and leaped in. Carter whirled in the motion of feinting back in the opposite direction to slice open the belly of the second man whose sword came down on empty air, his guts and blood pouring out across the ground. The second man already on his knees and dying, the tall leader frozen in mid-smile with his sword up to repel the feinted attack that never came, Carter stood five yards away, legs apart, sword out, watching the one man dying and the other a momentarily frozen statue.

The two attacking Siobhan made their moves at the same instant on some unseen signal. Unseen by anyone except Siobhan herself. In the split second between their standing poised and the swift motion of attack, her long samurai *katana* came off her shoulder and she darted sideways toward the attacker on the left. The swift, unexpected move, timed to take advantage of her opponent's force moving in the opposite direction, brought her behind the arc of his sword before he knew she had even moved, and out of the reach of the sword of the other attacker on her right.

The Australian plunged the *katana* into the attacker in front of her, withdrew as he dropped in a fountain of his own blood, and turned on the survivor feet apart, sword forward, in a duplication of Carter's stance.

The four faced each other, the two surviving black-robed attackers now aware they were not up against amateur swordsmen.

No one moved.

Shifted feet.

Watched.

Shuffled closer.

Held.

And the black-garbed attacker facing Siobhan broke first, rushing forward with a violent cry. His sword flashed down but sliced only empty air as the blood poured from the cut across his neck made by her faster sword that caught the final slash of his blade and twisted the sword from his already dead hands.

The tall leader strode forward. Carter met him. Their blades clashed, rang, flashed in the late evening sun, circled, and thrust. The tall leader of the attackers was a master swordsman. He parried all Carter's attacks but could make no headway against the skill of the Killmaster.

Siobhan came up behind the tall man in the black kimono. The man pivoted and backed toward the courtyard wall to keep them both in front of him.

"You've fought enough," Carter said.

The leader smiled. "I have two swords, American."

He continued to back toward the wall, and stumbled over the barely alive body of the first man Siobhan had cut down. Carter took the small opening, thrust and cut, and drew blood from the tall man's right arm and knocked away his *katana*.

With only his *wakizashi* in his left hand, the man nodded. "So?"

"You can't win now. Tell us who sent you," Carter said.

"No," the man said in English, pressing his bloody right arm against the black kimono. "I cannot win now. A pity. You are master swordsmen. I underestimated you both."

"It happens."

"I have failed my lord. You will both die soon. I shall merely be first."

Before they could move, the tall man slashed down with the *wakizashi* in both hands and decapitated his still twitching comrade, then cut his own throat in a single slash and fell to the courtyard, his blood spreading in a pool around him.

—From THE SAMURAI KILL
A New Nick Carter Spy Thriller
From Charter in July 1986

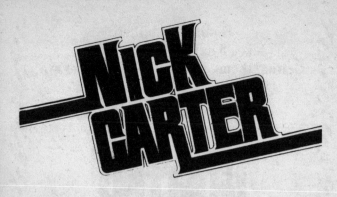

NICK CARTER

☐ 05386-6	**THE BERLIN TARGET**	$2.50
☐ 06790-5	**BLOOD OF THE SCIMITAR**	$2.50
☐ 57281-2	**BLOOD ULTIMATUM**	$2.50
☐ 06861-8	**THE BLUE ICE AFFAIR**	$2.50
☐ 57282-0	**THE CYCLOPS CONSPIRACY**	$2.50
☐ 14222-2	**DEATH HAND PLAY**	$2.50
☐ 21877-6	**THE EXECUTION EXCHANGE**	$2.50
☐ 57280-4	**THE KILLING GROUND**	$2.50
☐ 45520-4	**THE KREMLIN KILL**	$2.50
☐ 24089-5	**LAST FLIGHT TO MOSCOW**	$2.50
☐ 51353-0	**THE MACAO MASSACRE**	$2.50
☐ 52276-9	**THE MAYAN CONNECTION**	$2.50
☐ 52510-5	**MERCENARY MOUNTAIN**	$2.50
☐ 57502-1	**NIGHT OF THE WARHEADS**	$2.50
☐ 58612-0	**THE NORMANDY CODE**	$2.50
☐ 69180-3	**PURSUIT OF THE EAGLE**	$2.50
☐ 74965-8	**SAN JUAN INFERNO**	$2.50
☐ 79822-5	**TARGET RED STAR**	$2.50
☐ 79831-4	**THE TARLOV CIPHER**	$2.50
☐ 88568-3	**WHITE DEATH**	$2.50

Prices may be slightly higher in Canada.

Available at your local bookstore or return this form to:

 CHARTER
THE BERKLEY PUBLISHING GROUP, Dept. B
390 Murray Hill Parkway, East Rutherford, NJ 07073

Please send me the titles checked above. I enclose _____ Include $1.00 for postage and handling if one book is ordered; 25¢ per book for two or more not to exceed $1.75. California, Illinois, New Jersey and Tennessee residents please add sales tax. Prices subject to change without notice and may be higher in Canada.

NAME _____

ADDRESS _____

CITY _____ STATE/ZIP _____

(Allow six weeks for delivery.)

A8

**Finding them there
takes a new breed of courage.
Getting them out takes a new kind of war.**

M. I. A.
HUNTER

by Jack Buchanan

Trapped in a jungle half a world away,
they're men no one remembers — no one but former
Green Beret Mark Stone and the daring men who
join him. They're taking on an old enemy with
a new kind of war. And nothing is going to stop them
from settling their old scores.